MW00567954

If I Were Me

By The Same Author

A North American Education, 1973

Tribal Justice, 1974

Days and Nights in Calcutta, 1977

Lunar Attractions, 1979

Lusts, 1983

The Sorrow and the Terror, 1986

Resident Alien, 1986

Man and His World, 1992

I Had a Father, 1993

A NOVEL

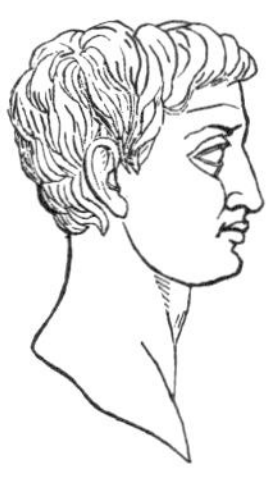

The Porcupine's Quill

CLARK BLAISE

CANADIAN CATALOGUING IN PUBLICATION DATA

Blaise, Clark, 1940-
If I were me : a novel

ISBN 0-88984-185-3

I. Title.

PS8553.L3413 1997 C813'.54 C97-930091-6
PR9199.3.B5213 1997

Published by The Porcupine's Quill, Inc., 68 Main Street, Erin, Ontario NOB 1TO, with financial assistance from The Canada Council and the Ontario Arts Council. The support of the Department of Canadian Heritage through the Book and Periodical Industry Development Programme is gratefully acknowledged.

Represented in Canada by the Literary Press Group. Trade orders are available from General Distribution Services.

The cover and author photographs are by Emma Dodge Hanson.

Readied for the press by John Metcalf. Copy edited by Doris Cowan. Typeset in Ehrhardt, printed on Zephyr Antique Laid, and bound at The Porcupine's Quill.

1 2 3 4 • 99 98 97

Inspired by, and dedicated to the memory of, Eli Mandel

Contents

PROLOGUE

Strangers in the Night

IN THE NIGHTS OF HIS FIFTIETH YEAR, before sleep, Lander was assaulted by faces. Every few minutes he opened his eyes for a reality check. Judy was breathing shallowly beside him, as she had for twenty years. The front wheel of her exercise bike splayed window light in a giant metal florette, like the barred metal blades of the dangerous rotating fans of his childhood that really could chop off a finger. His alpine ski machine gleamed expectantly, ready for him to climb aboard, its chrome neck stretched forward in a parody of earnestness. The partially opened closet door caught the red readout of the clock-radio display and spattered it against the full-length mirror on the door's inside surface. It was his room, indisputably, in this time, it was happening to his body within his experience, yet the moment he closed his eyes he was taken outside it.

The perfect ordinariness of the nighttime faces, their clarity and specificness, the lack of a single grotesque, or of spectacular beauty or familiarity, bespoke a kind of urgency that he could not ignore. Surely, if they sprang entirely from his own will, or existed for his own mild amusement, he would have remembered or invented faces of old friends, comforting icons or enemies, a few delicious women from his past or present. These were not staged faces, there was nothing coy, familiar or attractive. Or if attractive, mildly flawed. They reminded him of atelier faces, faces cherished for their typicalness or eccentricity, tossed off by a gifted master and his school. Life-like – there was no other word for them; he was being assaulted at night by an army of probable, interchangeable alternatives to the world he knew. He was sure that his faces were part of other people's lives, that he'd somehow crossed wires in this new fibre-optic universe, and was experiencing some neighbour's insomnia.

In Lander's intellectual tradition, Freud had taught him that dreams were urgent fragments of a ruptured past, personal and collective. They demanded attention, therapeutic resolution. Jung had taught, although Lander tried not to listen, that dreams were perfected futures, omens of uncompleted journeys.

A vast population had intersected his line of vision. They were not from his professional world. They were not American – if he could trust the flimsy evidence of haircuts and haberdashery – and many were not even European. Whenever he demanded their name or even a country, they faded, only to be replaced. Every night, he confronted a line-up of Latinos, Asians, Africans, middle-aged and old, male and female, poor and rich, like Roman busts, floating balloon-like above their own worlds, beyond speech, movement, or context, as though he were circulating in a vast professional cocktail party of tenured professors, without a proper invitation.

In the morning, or sometimes late at night, when he entered the visions in his notebook, as he habitually entered all his dreams and fantasies, he called them 'baseball cards'. A lavish pack of cards, shuffled and dealt by processes inside his skull, for mysterious purposes that he decided not to question. If he were to diagnose himself, he'd say he was going through a phase, he was part of something in development. There was no one he could share these half-sleeping adventures with. Judy, if wakened and informed, might have praised the interracial inclusiveness of his nighttime visitors, and the reassuring lack of younger women or troubled patients with robust transference problems. He'd learned years before not to discuss his patients with her, or to describe his research. He felt she was jealous of his involvement with patients, or at the very least that his emotions played a zero-sum game.

None seemed hostile. They seemed variants of probable faces, they reminded him, elusively, of names he couldn't place. They might have been the older brothers and sisters of people he knew well, parents even. They held still for a minute inspection, and he had the impression they were aware of him – as though they knew they were behind a one-way mirror. He wondered if this was the artist's 'fever of creativity', a tangible population of fully formed characters waiting for expression.

One night, in the crowd of nighttime faces, he saw a retreating figure, the broad, sloping shoulders and short legs, the fringe of curly hair. *You!* he cried with such force that Judy lurched beside him. The figure turned, reluctantly, as though apprehended in a theft, called to account. His double. Lander realized suddenly that he'd been waiting for it to happen. In his watered-down religious tradition, seeing one's double was not fatal. If anything, it was a sign of grace, the appearance of a personal genie.

The other Lander wore different glasses, and the jacket was unfamiliar, but it was Lander of the balding head and tadpole body, the sharp nose pulling against the flat planes of a Slavic face, a fuller beard than his, somewhat whiter. The bust was smiling, a little more accommodating than any who'd come before.

'That's right,' it said. 'You've found me. You're me.'

It was the first time a face had spoken.

'Where are you?' Lander asked. 'What is that place?'

He looked around, smiling, hands out in a familiar *can't-you-see?* gesture that reminded Lander of his father. 'This place?' he asked. In his double's world, there must have been props and other people and views out of windows, a common language, but none of it was available to Lander.

He spoke again. 'But I'm not you.'

By breakfast time, seeing himself at night slightly transformed seemed too small a thing to talk about, and Judy was too much involved in the inventory problems of the small boutique in a nearby shopping mall that she and two other women had opened. Both he and Judy were successful, which meant they had vast trust in each other, but little time, and their untended marriage was approaching a critical mass of unshared experience, uncommented upon, perhaps even unrealized. For the moment, they existed in the hollows and expectations each had carved out for the other.

Salad Days

'BY FIFTY, you have the face you deserve, the job you'll die at, the house they'll carry you out of ...' his father, the dry-cleaner, had insisted (then proved, at age fifty-five, from chain-smoking in a cloud of naphtha and acetone). Apart from his professional practice and his writing, Lander was involved with the reality of his mother's wasting away from Alzheimer's disease in a nursery home on the Yonkers side of Chappaqua. He tried to visit her a few hours every week, the first years as a dutiful, encouraging son, feeding her scraps of family information, safe memories, that might flush a response, a twitch of recognition. 'What a beautiful February morning,' he'd say, or, 'Wednesday, middle of the week.' Reality counseling, nurses called it, but if she answered, it might be a noun like 'bats' or 'butterfly', or a verb 'spilled' or 'swab', past tense or present, or any number of names of men and women he didn't recognize. '*Essie paint the chair*,' she said. She could not enjoy television, being unable to retain a plot, or even tolerate the intrusion of so many strangers. In the past year he'd been watching her slowly starve to death from an inability to recognize hunger or remember the taste of food, or to anticipate sweetness, heat, or cold, and finally, how to swallow. He watched her trying to communicate complicated ideas, judging from her frowns and gestures, before withdrawing; he watched her bat away food with her hands, swatting at the world like a baby. A world in which every second was intrusive, a world without context, life without antecedent or consequence. In the last several weeks, freed from all obligation to her, all guilt and the bonds of affection (he wished, profoundly, for her physical death) he'd begun thinking of his mother's silent dying not as personal loss, not as a philosophical vision of hell, but as a kind of clinical problem.

Still, Lander persisted. As a child of the Freudian method, he believed nothing issuing from the human mind was without form or purpose, particularly when others had declared it without merit or meaning. The one thing he could not imagine was meaninglessness. Alzheimer's word-salad was not random the way an infant's vocalizing might be. For Lander, the word 'salad' conformed to a recipe, words never lost their meaning, and locked inside the vault of language were his mother's own Dead Sea Scrolls.

He worried about '*Essie*', a name that recurred in her speech, but there had been no Essies in her life. Sadies, yes. Esthers, yes. *Painting the chair?* None of it made sense until another dream, this one of his mother, much younger, talking excitedly with a stranger. Lander strolled by, unrecognized, then suddenly became the stranger, his mother staring hard at him and speaking loudly. '*I say*,' she gestured, her arms flapping as though holding a brush and painting a wall, and Lander woke and stormed from his bed, writing out his vision in a fever of interpretation. *The chair* meant Lander himself, the person *in* the chair across from her. *Painting?* He hadn't a clue, except that it connected all her angers, her rage, at food being thrust at her, at strangers entering her room. Pain, perhaps, just plain pain. People thought of him as Freudian, unlocking meaning where there had been secrets. He thought of himself as Saussurean, a believer in the universality of language, its permanence, underlying all meaning and personality. He thought of Chomsky's theories, how language grows inside the brain, it is a human attribute, not a learned behaviour, and in the same parabolic function, language dies inside the brain, shedding its leaves, shrivelling. His mistake had been to look for content, for a woman named Essie, and for a special chair, and for a colour of paint, instead of approximate sounds. He was right, in that Alzheimer's had changed nothing of his mother, except that her content, her experiences, had become dead leaves. The leaves were still trying to speak.

Over her months, while language had persisted, he took notes. Then he recorded. The scraps of foreign language he took as an important clue – she was American-born, but she'd lived a life rich in others' languages, and she could at least make change and exchange pleasantries at the counter of the dry cleaning shop in five or six languages – it meant the words were not random, they belonged to her, they extruded from certain strata in her life. His mother couldn't locate herself in language; others in the nursing home who pressed Bibles on him, or hiked their skirts at the sight of any man, couldn't relate to society. *Oh, do watch the bed*, she'd say, *be a car and the cat won't slide, up the coffee hat and slippers too …*

He thought of his own occasional difficulties with names, or even at times with words, trying to apply his own common experience of word-retrieval, or name-recall, to his mother's problem with every sound and word in the universe. *It starts with 'M'*, and he began to wonder if the brain didn't store ideas as simple sounds, scanning a menu under the proper initial vowel or consonant, and then, by metre: it's a long word, tuh-dumm, tuh-dumm, an 'M' with three syllables, and then began throwing out words from his internal dictionary, like a computer's spell-check: Morrison? No, not quite. Then social history kicked in: Jewish, Wasp, Italian? Morrison? Mendelssohn. Menotti? The idea appealed with its model of the inherent humanness of memory and consciousness, linked with the inherent human gift of language. Cup could mean anything, but it didn't mean nothing, and before it stood for a concave object for holding tea, it probably meant a short word starting with 'c'.

Music, mathematics and poetry – sound, length and symbol – slid together as the primal organizers. Even a baby's vocalizing made new sense: it was opening up the verbal pathways, hitting on opening letters, intonation and word-length. And when finally, by accident, a sound was understood to be a word, fitting a concept or an object, it was retained, stored, and other words quickly jelled. It made sense. His mother had simply reversed the process of language acquisition, dropping the sorter, then the menu. There was a mind still working, but it had lost control of first letters, opening sounds, and the salad was an infinitely complex rhyming game. She still had the intonation and metres of normal speech but she'd lost control of syllables and second and third letters as well. There was no way of knowing if the mind behind the salad was aware of the loss. The doctors called Alzheimer's a blissful stage of total mental rest, language without consciousness. There was even doubt that she felt physical pain, with her lessened brain functions. At the brain clinic the specialist, studying her charts, had told Lander, 'It's lights out for the old girl. Look at the dead nodules. It's like a bombed-out city in there.'

To quiet his guilt, to answer the tragedy of his mother's dying – not a personal tragedy by this time, but the awareness that the loss of any individual was the loss of an entire branch of human history – Lander began the process of translation of his mother's last words. The strangest translation process in human history, a kind of calculus, not algebra, of translation, in which all terms were functions, not equivalents. There was no Rosetta stone, he was adrift in a world of familiar words much in the way Freud and Jung had wandered through the archetypes of dreams, each applying convenient meaning without the *click!* of final authority. Lander's mother had died, but her words – five hundred Alzheimer salad-words, translated into nearly three hundred pages of coherent text – became the basis of *Death Decoded: Language Acquisition and Language Loss*, a book, like the interpretation of dreams, that would link an everyday middle-aged event, memory-lapse with the continuum of language acquisition and language loss, the human process of birth and death. Some reviewers spoke of it as redemption; the first words from the Beyond. The dying still speak to us, nothing in human life is without relevance or meaning, we are human till the last breath is taken from us.

Harsher critics saw it as last-gasp yuppyism, baby-boomer possessiveness, vigorous middle age staking a claim even to old age and death. 'Gerald Lander, 51-year-old clinical psychologist, the sage of Chappaqua, boldly goes where no one has gone before,' wrote one detractor in the *New York Times Book Review*, 'claiming to have walked to the very portals of eternity. His translation of his mother's terminal babble is a curious labour of love and *hubris*, more a claim for his own immortality than a rendering of near-death experience. With his debts to Sigmund Freud all too obvious, Lander should be reminded of his master's words: "Sometimes a cigar is just a cigar." As harsh as it may seem to a humanist of Lander's obvious compassion, sometimes gibberish, even a beloved mother's gibberish, is just noise. For God's sake, let the elderly die in peace. There is, after all, a limit to what children might own of their parents, what the all-consuming present might seize of a parent's present agony and private past. Despite today's publishing climate, and the Wall Street mentality that fuels it, not everything can be – or should be – turned to vast profit.'

The latter; apparently, was a reference to Lander's surprise appearance – considering the difficult and uncompromising language of the book, as well as his own unglamorous self – for fifty straight weeks at the top of the world's bestseller lists. In international publishing circles, his name became linked with the improbable trio of other accidental bestsellers, Umberto Eco, Stephen Hawking and Salman Rushdie.

A Saint

MY SON HAD GRADUATED from college in Oregon, and I was on the way back to my midwestern life. A poet had delivered the graduation speech. I took pleasure in his words: *a baby tiger, just born, has an ox-eating spirit*. He did not mean, in the way of successful alumni addressing sleek young graduates, to leap upon the backs of oxen, though many seemed to take it that way. He meant for us to approach the world respectful of variety and of necessity, he meant to contrast appearance and appetite. My boy and I ate under a tent and listened to the projects of the new graduates around us, and to their proud parents. We watched the intact parental units dance to an orchestra, then the older successful men and much younger wives dance convincingly to the wives' music, and we left early. My boy had been happy there, had drifted into a counter-cultural community. He had no project in mind except escape, and though pleasant to everyone, hated his classmates. A friend once said of him, ah, Sagittarian. It is their nature to be adult in childhood, and childish in maturity. He seemed to be on course, and I wished him well. It was the traditional leave-taking of a father to a son: I have raised you, inculcated you, educated you, warned you, encouraged you, sent you every conflicting signal in the universe. You were in my arms for a couple of years, in my hands for five or six, in my house for a dozen more. You're bigger than me, stronger, you can slay an ox.

At the airport, I had noticed the woman in the waiting room. I sit in the smoking section though I don't smoke. In general, I prefer people who smoke, ox-eaters, fragile predators like cats. Maureen O'Hara on a bad day, I thought, green eyes – dating myself, like old guys dancing with younger women, like men my age with toddlers by the punch bowl. A honey-roasted blonde, lumberjack shirt and faded jeans, a backpack. Maureen O'Hara on a bad day, or a distracted day with the beacon of her beauty slightly broken, is better than Maureen O'Hara on a good day, when her helpless beauty could only bear down on you.

There would be no story if fate had not put us together in 10A and B. Her name was Patty, her husband in Richmond went by the name of Terry. And she was returning to Richmond, a city she hated, from a ten-day camping trip with six male friends from Boston College. One of them said, 'This is what movies are made of.' My *Big Chill*, she said, Terry couldn't come. Too busy making the President's Golden Circle, writing up a million dollars in policies for the fifth straight year. She'd been married ten years, with him thirteen.

Her story is racing ahead, I want to slow it down. There are women who somehow make you feel and act and talk better than you are; others, much worse, even when they are the source of all your inspiration. Patty, whom I will never see again, is among the first. Two minutes with her, and I intuited nearly everything about her. Maybe not the four children, but the wistfulness about some briefly opened door, some recent transcendence. You were an actor, I said, quite confidently and It wasn't my intuition, it was her actor's radiance. Only some soaps, she said. I did soaps to pay for more acting and singing and dancing lessons. An agency sent me to Atlanta for some Coke ads. Three weeks for one of those Teach the World to Sing jobbies and I met Terry – he was in theatre then. He saw me in an ad and called the agency. I was thrilled. I acted in once of his plays. His father had an insurance agency in Richmond, and two years later the father died, and Terry ...

Nothing happened in Oregon, she said. I don't want you to get the wrong impression.

But something did, I said.

I was raped in Richmond. Can you imagine, living alone in Boston and New York all those years, hanging out with models and actors, living in Hell's Kitchen, and I get raped in a parking garage in Richmond? I knew the name of every guy hanging out on the stoops on Forty-fourth between Tenth and Broadway. I was a soft touch, I gave them money, I talked with them, I got them tickets to some of my shows. They would have died for me, and I know she's telling the truth, she is the sort that some men would kill for, some die for, but Terry would kill her if something had happened in Oregon.

Defending Your Life, I said, overcoming fear, doubt, insecurity is what separates men from angels. I'd seen *Wings of Desire* a few weeks earlier, and I saw through her with such clarity I almost said: Patty, it's no accident we're sitting together. I am the man put here to listen to you. But I'm not a man. I was killed in a BMW crash two weeks ago, and you're my first case since I was sent down. Somewhere over Utah I said, 'A lot of men will be returning to their wives as dissatisfied with their marriages as you are.'

One of them said, 'Life has big plans for you. Don't close it off.'

You love this man, don't you, Patty.

I want to go back to New York, but one of these men – he lives in the woods, sort of a conservationist – he hates the city. He never married, he's a kind of soulmate. Knows the trails, knows what to eat, what to avoid. I feel safe with him, even in the woods. I don't feel safe in Richmond with all my cars and memberships. He says I'm closing my life. I lay in his arms at night – nothing happened – but I slept in ways I've never slept before, like a baby, with dreams I didn't want to leave.

One day, I was taking a bath in the river near the campsite and I didn't know the men were all watching me. They didn't tell me till we were sitting around the campfire and they started exchanging opinions on how I could improve my looks, starting out with my hair, or something, and then getting more and more intimate, you know, and I'm starting to get redder and redder. I mean, four kids, and thirty-six, you're not going to turn on many guys, especially not buck naked in a snow-fed stream.

A true angel, perhaps, would have kissed her then, or would have said like Willie Nelson if you don't want my peaches, baby, then why you shake my tree? Or he might have given up immortality on the spot, traded omniscience and invisibility for mutable, ecstatic flesh, moist members moving, and all its agony. A *Penthouse* fell out of one man's backpack, why do men buy it, is seeing pictures really more pleasurable than a woman's body? *Ever watch Dockers ads on television, I ask. Beer ads?* It was the only question I couldn't ask, I felt he was measuring those girls against me in the river and I didn't measure up, I'm all saggy, I've got a little roll, and Christ if my legs were bananas they'd be selling at half price. Well, you're a man, you've probably noticed it's downhill pretty fast from my eyes, but my eyes, I mean they need some shadow and all but I've still got a bit of it, don't I? Men were always in my power. Professors were in my power. God, this is awful, even priests, all the laps I sat in – we only hear about priests and little boys, but believe me, the Church isn't all that sick.

Patty, I said, you are beautiful, your eyes are the colour of thin caramel glaze over a crisp green apple and thoughts of your body rising from the waters leave me aghast with pleasure. You still have it, you are exactly halfway between my son and me, but life doesn't have any more big plans for you, maybe only one medium-sized one.

Leap, Saint Patty. I present myself to you like a tethered bull in a pasture. Rip my stupid throat out.

Kristallnacht

THEIR SHOES MADE LOVE all night at the foot of the stairs, where they had kicked them off. In the bright early light the next morning he prowled her kitchen, looking for the cat food in her unreadable language. He'll remember the kitchen, the words on cat food labels – in German, Polish or Czech, and Serbo-Croatian, he couldn't tell – and where she kept the can-opener and his pride in not disturbing her, more, perhaps, than he'll remember the night before, the kicking off of the shoes, the famished rush to a bed before they magnetized the moon. He'll remember it all as something unexpected and undeserved. Maybe it could not have happened in another week, might never have happened a year before, or even a few months later. They'd clung to each other like Londoners in the blitz, seeking dark in the sunlit night, safety in her wooden cottage.

Out on the street in the white summer nights, prowling gangs controlled the city. No guns, the violence was more intimate; chains swung in an arc then down on a skull, tire irons clanking down the brick streets, echoing off the pastel canyons of Hanseatic housing. Blond young men in American T-shirts and blue jeans, squatting in the middle of ancient roads, holding their split-open heads as blood trickled between their fingers.

For her, perhaps, he was the man who appeared in her life in the weeks before history ended. He is the man she chose because he was new, and innocent, and somehow impervious to the local tragedies. A man who could appreciate her memories, she said, as she lifted crystal wine glasses from a satin-lined little casket with its Gothic lettering and swastika imprint, inside a carved-oak settee, the heavy furniture of the independence era, the glasses of the Nazi occupation, and poured the Moldavian wine of the dying present. 'This wine is too sweet,' she said, 'they can't do anything right,' toasting his glass nevertheless. Can you imagine these Germans, she asked, even in the War, even losing the War, turning out crystal so pure, so fine, that *trocken Auslese* could not be poured into the lighter *Rheinwein* glasses – too sweet, too heavy, you know – or else the *prosit!* would not chime?

They toasted each sip, and the sips lasted for hours.

He had stood all afternoon in line with her for pork, or rather the fat of pork, to make a broth for eggs she'd traded and vegetables from her garden. It had not seemed like three hours, though he realized it was privilege speaking, being the friend, the lover, of a beautiful woman – and she was that, dramatically so, with pale skin stretched over perfect bones, under her absurdly garish Romanian scarf – rare privilege being inducted for a day or two into the intimacies of her life, learning the only words in her language that he would ever have to know, some nouns for vegetables, some verbs for slicing them, some soaps, some nonexistent meat, anaemic cheese and watered milk, some endearments for a child coming home from school and finding a strange man in his mother's kitchen – there have been so many, she said, it doesn't matter except that you talk to him, show some interest, he's studying English, you know, and he likes to practise – and some verbs and nouns of intimacy, conferring a kind of giddy mastery that no classroom had ever taught.

They'd taken buses, and then a tram, though taxis hooted when they saw him, guessing his foreignness, shouting out entreaties, then threats in the nearest Western languages, descending from Finnish to German and finally Hungarian. Under the awnings of darkened stores, girls in leather skirts pushed their hips into him, boys in leather jackets with metal studs waited nearby on their bicycles. Two years before, the girls had been in high school preparing for college, their pimps had been playing football and trying to dodge the draft.

She would not permit herself the luxury of a cab ride, which she said she associated with visits to her mother in a bad part of town, near the public housing developments where the Tadzhiks and Uzbeks stayed, close to the barracks where Tatars manned a rim of tanks and anti-aircraft batteries, for protection against the likes of him. Decent women under seventy were not safe in those areas, where satellite dishes brought in Western television, and drunken bachelor Asians watched *Miami Vice*. 'But let me spend this money,' he said. 'I want to spend something on you, I want to make your life a little better.' It would be unspeakable to leave with a wad of rubles in his pocket, those worthless rubles that would have cost him a month's salary just a year before. 'Please,' he'd begged, 'you can use this, it's six months' salary for you.' She'd stepped briskly ahead while cabbies whistled, then she turned. 'Next, you'll want to take me to your hotel,' she said.

She had her pride, he learned that night, with her well-behaved boy speaking well-drilled English, and with the amazing soups of sour cream and rhubarb, potatoes and beets, pork fat, dill and eggs, rye bread and Moldavian wine in crystal Nazi glasses. Later, in bed: if you wish, you can send me books, she said, when you get back to your country. Books used to be stolen in the mail, but now it doesn't matter. And send me magazines. *Lear's,* she said, and *Apartment Living*, and maybe *California*. Oh, and some cat food.

He is in her kitchen, and a ginger cat rubs her whiskers on his naked leg. Just a minute, Sasu, he says. She, if it is a she, eats an egg, lightly whisked, in sour cream, lightly watered. In this country, house-cats eat as well as foreign lovers. To a man, all cats are female: graceful, elusive, mysterious, and to a woman, they're always male: competent, agile, undemanding.

Is that a wad of rubles, or are you just glad to see me? Dear Abby: how does a gentleman leave the equivalent of twenty thousand dollars on a lady's bed without arousing undue suspicion over motives or morals, averting hostility or an international incident? The thought occurs to him: *this was all for her cat!* then he dismisses it, almost. Does it matter? And how will an American, ugly or beautiful, ever know?

He pulls out the settee drawer, the little sarcophagus of wine glasses nestled inside the Nazi shroud, and tucks every ruble and kopeck into a satin cavity where one glass, over the years, must have broken. He holds up a glass and raps it gently with his fingernail: *T-i-i-n-g!* and remembers the thunk of bicycle chains and the clanging of tire irons hurled down an empty street. It is the high, pure note of collective memory. He feels he has lived fifty years in two days and a night. The walls are down, the currency is melting, and he mounts the stairs wondering if there are not more ways than this of celebrating.

Drawing Rooms

AFTER HIS TALK TO THE CITY COUNCIL, Lander and Jerzy Adamowicz, the assistant commissioner, took their brandies on the balcony outside the council chambers. If you can believe it, Dr Lander, this was once a prosperous city, before the war and before the Communists, Adamowicz was saying. As a distinguished visitor in a time of tumultuous transformation, Lander had been asked to contribute to a 'post-Communist urban dialogue'. He'd chosen this city in western Poland not just for its renowned medical college, where he'd conducted a seminar on his theories of language and memory, but to visit the town his family had come from.

Inside the council chambers, hollowed out from the splendour of an old private mansion, the walls had been hung with tourist posters of Gdansk and Krakow, Vilna, Riga, Smolensk and Minsk, Lvov, Pskov and Tatra mountains. All rather revanchist, the AC had admitted, as though the old Polish-Lithuanian Confederation were trying to re-establish itself now that the Russians were in retreat. The hallways and smaller bedrooms of the mansion were a warren of tiny offices with hastily erected drywall partitions, each whining with dot-matrix printers and fax machines. Lander had thought of the house as a schema of the brain itself, Polish liberation like a brain, recovering from a stroke. Being in the middle of it was a privilege.

The dominant landmark, of course, was the cathedral. Next, on a hilltop, the college and hospital. The Communist Party headquarters with its unilluminated red star was boarded up, with squatter families occupying the ground floor. There were the usual Stalinist sports palace and playing field, islands of ghostly concrete and patches of scruffy grass. Just below the balcony, in a tiny park, families of refugee Ukrainians and gypsies had spread quilts between tree branches, and propped up boards and cardboard slabs for a semblance of privacy.

'We were close enough to Germany in those pre-war years for a fanning out of German wealth and a taste for Mozart,' said

Adamowicz, but remote enough not to dilute basic Polish decency. *Here you stand on the heart of Pomeranian-Polish culture, Dr Lander*, the place where Slavic Catholicism and Prussian Protestantism merged. And Jewish, too, of course, he'd quickly added, Jews supplying soul to the Germans and quickness to the Poles (quickness? Lander wondered), qualities now lost forever. 'We used to be the most cosmopolitan country in Europe. Now we're ninety-nine percent Catholic and ninety-nine percent Polish. We've been made stupid by history. How this country has suffered, Dr Lander!'

It had proven an ideal location for a cosmopolitan city, with its own Grand Canal linking the Baltic ports with the Oder and Berlin. The present-day canal wove through the foulest and most congested part of the city like a dirty string. The city council planned to dredge the canal and clean the waters, to rebuild the old promenade, to raze and rehabilitate derelict buildings and lease them to Benetton, McDonald's and Mövenpick.

In the council chambers, Lander had spoken against demolition. All things seemed possible in the new eastern Europe, why not a revolution of the soul? The best of all traditions – local, European, capitalist, socialist – seemed within reach. He'd suggested turning over the abandoned buildings rent-free to artists, dancers, weavers and publishers, for coffee-houses and cheap restaurants, printing presses, theatres and cinemas, subject to the tenants themselves doing all renovation. Charge rent only after they succeeded. Nothing makes an area more attractive, and more valuable, than a concentration of creative people. He'd felt he was being persuasive until he mentioned enlisting German aid. Council faces had drooped, eyes looked down, a few councillors had shaken their heads.

The town council had presented him with a gift book of Pomeranian etchings, circa 1910, featuring urban views of the prosperous old city. The cathedral, much as it was today; Sternfeld's Department Store, with families streaming in and out; parks, trams, and the opera house; a synagogue, baths and the Lutheran *Heiligekirche*, all of which had disappeared. Eighty years earlier, the canal had defined the center of a compact, orderly city. The promenade was edged by trees along the waterside, like Amsterdam. Sidewalk cafés invited strollers. The shaded walks led to theatres and to the opera house, past docks tied up with decorated rowboats.

'They were such pigs, the Communists,' said Adamowicz, with sudden passion. He'd been trained in Australia, where local English had worked small wonders on his vowels. 'Communists were bysically pay-sants who took revenge on the city. They tore down the landmarks. They stuffed farm families into these old city houses, family after family. They hated everything the city stood for.' *Like Jews,* thought Lander. 'Culture, values, property, wealth, beauty – all of it had to get beaten down. That was the dirty war inside of Communism. Everything to humiliate the past, replace it with trash – out of vain-geance, not principle. How we suffered.'

'And the Germans are out, definitely?' Lander had been prepared to say that inviting German investment need not imply forgiveness. Germany was the nearest source of hard currency; logically speaking, they shouldn't be ignored.

'Pay-sants say pigs may stink but you can still eat pork. The pig is part of God's creation. We still don't know about Germans.'

Lander respected Poland's long memory. He trusted Jerzy Adamowicz. He had found a man he could stand on a balcony with, not having to talk.

His maternal great-grandparents, the Sternfelds, ghetto-sprung businessmen who'd educated their sons and daughters in Germany and France, had built a substantial residence – brick with white marble trim, on the London model – somewhere in this city, in the middle of an elegant block facing a private park. As a child in a third-floor Brooklyn flat, Lander has spent hundreds of hours staring at pictures of the house and of a little girl, his grandmother, tended by a nurse, riding a high-wheeled bicycle. Two old touring cars, with chauffeurs in livery, were parked in front of an unimaginably fine mansion, something belonging in Park Slope or the tree-lined brownstones of East Side Manhattan. Evidence, in Lander's helter-skelter New World, of having come from somewhere, 'from People', as his mother put it, of having had something substantial to lose.

No one in the current city council remembered such a park, or row of brownstones, although everyone revered the Sternfeld name. At the turn of the century, Sternfeld's Department Store was importing English porcelain, Paris fashions, Dutch cheese and German technology. Sternfeld agents, smart boys who'd married into the family, scouted every European city for quality and value, turning Sternfeld's into the biggest store between Berlin and Warsaw, and maybe the finest store of any kind between Vienna and Stockholm.

Before she'd lost her ability to remember, or to communicate, Lander's mother had spoken proudly of her mother's childhood with its loyal Polish servants, horses stabled in the country, piano lessons and recitals, tea and cakes served in the drawing room. *Drawing room* was something Lander associated with Sigmund Freud or Sherlock Holmes: ... *showing the distraught young woman into my drawing-room ... Show the good inspector into my drawing-rooms, Watson ...* Even today the phrase evoked a cool, secretive, cavelike seriousness; a heavy velvet splendour in dark walnut trim where mysterious rituals were enacted. A place unseen, mysterious, but deeply felt, like the human mind itself.

One day in 1902 the Sternfelds had gathered in the drawing-room and submitted to a portrait photographer, an afternoon's vanity that became the only lasting proof of their ever having existed. The son in the picture was his great-uncle Henryk in a white student cap, on a visit from the medical faculty in Berlin. The three lively, dimpled daughters stood behind their bald, bearded father, whose one arm rested on a small table draped in fringed damask. One of those girls married the Vilna agent, came to New York, and became Lander's grandmother. His great-grandmother, almost frail and scholarly, with a Talmudist's face unreplicated among her children, seemed to be the only Sternfeld looking beyond that day, out of the drawing room into the future.

After Berlin, Henryk Sternfeld had gone to Vienna, become an apostle of Freud and set up the first psychoanalytic practice in western Poland. Sternfeld meant *field of stars*, and he'd used a starry comet-tail as an informal family crest on personalized stationery. As a wise, Freud-circle elder, he had lectured at Columbia in the year of Lander's birth, shmoozed with his old Berlin and Vienna colleagues at the New School, and turned down an offer to remain in New York. He'd found the city too trashy and Italian for his tastes. Henryk Sternfeld preferred 'Don Giovanni' to 'Aida', Furtwangler to Toscanini. *I could not live in a country who listens to such a posturing little monkey without complaining,* he wrote on his field of stars, thanking his relatives: his widowed sister, her cultivated daughter and civil-servant husband, and their baby son, for hospitality in a Depression-dimmed, cluttered Brooklyn flat.

Lander's mother had a special name – Heinrich, sometimes just Heinie – for her famous uncle.

In 1937 the great man, his wife, family, grandchildren and servants returned to Poland on first-class tickets. The return trip was curiously uncrowded. The captain's table was open to them every night, champagne was pressed upon them from breakfast till bedtime. The orchestra played all their favourite tunes. He was interviewed at dockside about the future of Freud's revolution in America, which he considered dubious, and their New York purchases were whisked through customs.

On *Blutsonntag*, September 3, 1939, when the German forces swept across Pomerania, all the Polish schoolteachers and doctors, all the professors, students and college graduates, every man with education, every unionist, artist, priest, communist, every nationalist, every politician, every policeman, every gypsy and Jew, every defective, every mental patient was taken to the back wall of the cathedral and shot. Thirty thousand died that Sunday, in actions that lasted from first Mass till after dark, the white-bearded analyst in his British tweeds – teacher, doctor, professor, nationalist, Jew – at the top of every list.

As a child, Lander had felt the same connection to the field of nighttime stars that he did, as a grown-up, to drawing-rooms, and as just minutes earlier as he had to the Pomeranian etchings. The feeling was smallness, of standing alone on a hill in the dark, looking up. It was a feeling of wonder, close to exquisite heartbreak. Those families in the etchings under the umbrellas eating their ice cream staring at the canal could have been his, but they'd become stars, eighty light-years away. There had been a rupture in history, like his mother's memories and her ability to communicate them; nothing but shreds could be retrieved.

He turned slowly from the city view, then stared down at the dusty park studded with tree-stumps where refugee families were lighting their fires, and the string of dented Polish Fiats parked in the narrow street below him, then looked back over his shoulder into the empty council chambers. He realized suddenly where he was standing. Adamowicz drew closer, as though to help a stricken man. He recognized it now, everything. This is the balcony, underlined with dingy marble trim, that his grandmother had stood on, waving down to servants, looking out on an urban forest. The block of mansions had been destroyed. Wood mouldings and paintings had been carried out or burned, books and records destroyed, mezuzahs ripped from the doorframes. He felt he had suffered a stroke. He gripped the iron railings of the balcony and held on until the roaring in his ears, the swirl of images, the weakness in his body subsided.

The Banality of Virtue

THE LETTER WAS WAITING at his Warsaw hotel. 'When you're in Gdansk, why not come to dinner in Sopot?' It was signed Tewfiqa and Slava. The hopeful sign was the greeting: *Dear Daddy*. Gdansk was on his government-arranged, Baltic itinerary, before Helsinki and Stockholm, after Bydgoszcz and a few other vowel-challenged provincial cities.

So: Rachel still noted his presence, perhaps even cared. At Wellesley, she'd started out a Black studies major, dropped out at the end of her junior year, worked a year in a Roxbury daycare centre, then enrolled at Hunter in Russian. Then graduate research ('It Ain't Just Pushkin: The African Presence in 19th-century Russia') had taken her to Moscow during perestroika. Knowing Russian isn't just a refinement, like French or Italian; it's a vocation, it becomes your life. You can write your ticket. As a Russian-speaking African-American woman with a suburban accent and social skills, she'd been offered places in business, in government, in the media, none of which had interested her. Rejection spoke well of her character, Lander had thought, her eventual prospects.

On a trip to Tashkent she'd married a Russian named Pyotr Shvartz, making her a real *shvartze* – what's new – she'd joked. They planned to return to the States, but when consular investigators swept through their apartment on a surprise visit, they found that Pyotr had left on an extended trip to the Caucausus with no forwarding address. The apartment contained no evidence of his underwear, no cigarette butts, no vodka – none of the sweet nothings of international courtship. The Shvartzes could not satisfy minimal standards of intimacy to warrant immigration through marriage. They called themselves Jews, but Pyotr knew no rituals and abhorred the very idea of Israel. ('I've been surrounded by Muslims all my life,' he'd said). She claimed Jewishness despite appearances, even reciting from the *haftara* and taking out pictures of her elaborate Chappaqua *bat-mitzvah* ten years earlier. Rachel had always taken to rituals. 'You don't look very comfortable in those pictures,' the official had noted.

Like many people in that time and place, the young Landers had felt their personal distaste for the war in Vietnam, and their country's failure to fight for racial justice at home, called for an act of positive, lifelong commitment. The prevailing ethos dictated: think globally, act locally; save one child and you've saved the world; if you're not part of the solution, you're part of the problem. They were liberal, concerned, suburban young professionals – *yuppie* had not yet been invented – Lander a clinical psychologist with academic connections in the city, and Judy just beginning to interest herself in the women's movement. She was debating a return to school – law, perhaps, or local politics.

One Sunday she did the unthinkable, threw the *Times* across the living room, tore up the 'Magazine' section and the 'Book Review', ripped the rabbit ears from the back of the television set and jerked the cord from its socket. 'I want to deface something!' she screamed. 'I want to scratch my name on the Lincoln Memorial. I want to blow something up!' Lander thought she was acting out, jealous of his life in the city and some early success, behaving badly, being just a little bratty. Like Lander, she was ready for a tango with the Zeitgeist.

He made the not unreasonable suggestion – in that time and place – that they look into adopting a baby. Judy had lost pregnancies in the third and fourth months; she couldn't tolerate a third. If you did observable good in removing an innocent life from hopeless conditions and resolving your own problems in the bargain, you were fulfilling the injunctions of the age. What fiercer act of good faith, of commitment, of engagement?

And so they pondered their choices: black, native American, Third World. Interracial adoptions were considered noble. Black parents couldn't take white or Asian babies, nor could they keep up with the avalanche of orphaned or abandoned black babies. The Landers never looked for children of their faith, or interracial children offered by Jewish orphanages. Although Lander was just a generation removed from the Holocaust, he and Judy were non-observant suburbanites for whom 'Jewish' was little more than a default position. He felt Jewish more strongly than he felt Other; it felt more a statement of what he was not than of what he was.

At the adoption agency the baby girls had been dressed in pink flannel nighties with pink ribbons in their nappy hair; the boys in T-shirts with cute, snarly sayings or team logos. Some of the girls were obviously bright, affectionate and pretty, potential Diana Rosses reaching out for an audience. But the Landers had wanted a damaged baby. They'd wanted a baby through whom the American holocaust had swept. They found her in a corner crib, still as a loaf of pumpernickel, wrapped in pink. She whimpered but didn't cry. The whimpering didn't change pitch or intensity even when she was picked up and held. Heroin, the nurse explained. Autistic, Lander thought. She's mourning something, said Judy. When the agency cautioned against taking her, of all the baby girls in the nursery, Judy clung to her even more tightly. She might never recover from the drugs in her blood, from suspect genes, the trauma of her delivery, the loss of a finger (they hadn't noticed) from frostbite. She'd been found in the garbage, not even wrapped in rags or a blanket. How could they resist? The whole world would go into her making.

Rachel (as they named her) did recover, even from the loss of a finger and the scattering of dead spots on her toes and the rim of one ear. They took extra care to wrap her warmly in the winter. She was slow in developing, at least by the standards of Chappaqua, but the Montessori school practically sent a limousine daily to pick her up – their only black child – and by three she had passed subtle developmental tests that indicated she was average or at least not handicapped. Average was not acceptable in the Lander house; the school allowed that she might even be slightly above average. As her suburban childhood progressed she was given the full range of skating and dance lessons, she learned to play the piano – passably, given the one-finger handicap – and a variety of stringed instruments.

Lander's father, a pants-presser turned dry-cleaner, had a low opinion of a *shvartze* granddaughter. Not race exactly, to which he was more indifferent than tolerant, but the sheer visual inappropriateness. The mismatch – how to explain her running around behind the counter when she was in the laundry? Who would push her in the stroller in the park and do the explaining? Rachel at six and seven messed up his ticket-recall system – his last great extravagance, his pride, the automated pulley-chain – in his laundry. She loved to watch a thousand shirts and suits march along an overhead track, emerge like trains from a tunnel and stop precisely at the cash register in her grandmother's hand. Lander's father would slap her hand. It costs, he said, each press of the button is like an elevator going up three stories. It was Lander's mother who put her on her lap and let her punch in each customer's ticket.

One summer day when Rachel, then seven, was playing in the front yard, Judy noticed something disturbing although she did not know exactly how to cope with it – or when, or if – to intervene. An old black woman shabbily dressed in an overcoat and watch-cap stood in the Lander yard talking to their daughter. Judy thought at first, I shouldn't disturb them. They must seem miraculous to one another. She's probably a maid in the neighbourhood, Judy rationalized, except that maids were better dressed and younger and would never be allowed to wear an out-of-season overcoat. By the time Judy got to the front door the old woman had seized Rachel and begun shaking her by the shoulders. Before she could intervene the old woman had reduced the girl to tears. 'Your name is Miz Lander? I believe you have stolen my granddaughter, Amber. I was just telling her about her real mama. And I don't reckon she's ever going to forget.'

Judy, ashamed of her reaction for the rest of her life, abandoned them both and ran inside and called the police, saying there's a horrible woman attacking my child who must be removed. Later she thought of it as the moment that ended Rachel's childhood and turned her from their daughter into something they always feared was present, like a hidden genetic malfunction that would take its time but surely announce itself. By the time Judy returned to her daughter the old woman had left and the girl had regained her composure and announced, 'My real mama's name is Latasha and she loves me and she's sleeping in heaven tonight but dreaming of me.'

They never saw the old woman again, yet they felt she had marked their house and was keeping them under some sort of surveillance. She noticed young black men – uncles? cousins? – in parked cars at the corner. Judy walked Rachel to school and picked her up until she got old enough to demand a bit of privacy. Rachel did appear to be naturally athletic, taller, faster, stronger, compared to most of the girls in high school and to poor myopic Sam ('Sam Lander the Salamander,' Rachel would call him), their son born five years later. Though the Landers tried to turn her away from the easy clichés of track and basketball, or discouraged coaches who salivated at the prospect of a fast-twitch princess on their team, she nevertheless excelled in sports and studies. In that ninety-percent-white, nine-percent-Asian suburban school, she was popular: Homecoming Queen, three-sport captain, the lone black face in various activities and honour societies, naturally gifted in music and languages, Harvard early-admittee, popular with boys.

But Amber, or her reincarnations, had never died. When Rachel was eleven, attending a two-week summer camp, Lander had received an urgent call. 'Dr Lander, this is Tewfiqa's crafts teacher. We have to talk.'

'I'm a clinician, Mrs Tatum. What seems to be the girl's problem?'

'The girl, Dr Lander, carries a knife. She threatens everyone.'

'That's very disturbing – wait, has she harmed Rachel?'

'Rachel? Rachel, Dr Lander? I'm talking about Tewfiqa. My God –'

Back in the German times, when Danzig was the free city, Sopot had been a high bourgeois resort close enough for business, removed enough for graciousness. Up the coast was Königsberg, now Russian Kaliningrad, the capital, the city of philosophers and musicians, one-time cosmopolis of the Baltic. Further north, Riga, ancient home of Lander's paternal side. A few hundred miles west in Lübeck and several lifetimes earlier, Tonio Kröger had admired Hans Hansen and Ingeborg Holm and splashed upon the beach. German Danzig had been the city of Günter Grass; Polish Gdansk was the city of Pawel Huelle and the shipyards, Lech Walesa and the fall of Communism. Across the waters came Helsinki Watch and the Nobel Prizes. Lander approved of the Baltic. Something appealed to him about the cold, septic, eel-torn Baltic – now a toxic dump, its fumes sealed by oil slicks. It seemed to have an admirable, civilizing effect on a dozen disparate people. Unlike, say, the Mediterranean.

Even today, Sopot retained a bit of charm, some faded pastel on the stucco and wood trim, narrow streets following the ancient dunes of a wilder, cleaner Baltic coast, low buildings with language-school placards in the second-floor windows. Nowadays Sopot had its own identity as a distant suburb, far from the city's swirl.

Her name was on the door, just as she'd warned him: *Tewfiqa Niggadyke*. He spent a long time looking at it before ringing the bell. How dare she, his daughter, his New World Lander, his atonement. Don't get in a panic, she'd warned him. Here, they think it's Dutch.

He'd made a scene, holding the phone and a bouquet of flowers in the Gdansk train station. She'd given him directions, she'd been warm and funny, then she threw him her new name. 'Of all the insults,' he'd cried. 'I won't visit you. That's not a name, it's a vanity plate.'

'I didn't expect you to understand,' she'd said.

'Don't hand me that past tense, that "didn't expect" like you *always* knew. I understand perfectly. You want the world to pay attention to you. What's not to understand?'

'And you don't?' she'd countered.

'I never said respect. I said attention.'

'Well, forgive me if I'm a simple English teacher. Did you ever think this respect you've earned makes it very hard for someone like me to have to share your name?'

Slava was small, not ignorant and substantial the way Lander had been raised to think of Polish women. If anything, she seemed frail and scholarly, her hair chewed and blondish, glasses overlarge, ears prominent, teeth bad. She earned her living by translating French and German books and investment guides and how-to's for new profit-minded Polish publishers.

'Slava was the Polish translator of Cixous and Kristeva and Christa Wolf. Now they only send her crap. I'm teaching her English so we can collaborate on Toni Morrison,' Tewfiqa explained. His daughter had become the Pole: wide, strong, assertive.

They had three rooms, painted in red and blue and green enamels – a medley of Popsicle colours that made you think of licking the walls – a kitchen alcove with a sink and a propane campstove with an oven hood, a small refrigerator; a bed-sitting-dining room with Indian bedspreads and a round table, and a small study with a paint-flecked desk and an old schoolroom chair which overlooked Sopot's main street. Slava tended flower-boxes and hanging ferns, they had a cat, an aquarium, Polish movie posters, a stereo, and stacks of books that had outgrown various attempts at bookcases. On the small dining table, rescued, it would appear, from the same schoolhouse, they had arranged a bottle of wine, a ham, a bowl of greens, another of noodles. Suddenly he was back in 1955, in his undergraduate student apartment in Hyde Park, the details so inevitable, so poignant, it was almost as though he'd described it to Rachel in his memories and she'd transcribed it.

Rachel – strike that, Tewfiqa, the Russian scholar – earned her living teaching English in a country that had rejected its last word of Russian six years before. It wasn't easy, being black, despite having a U.S. embassy English teaching certificate. Polish businessmen took one look at her and asked, how can an African person know English? This is a joke, surely. They saw NBA games and black movies and heard rap – they knew that wasn't English. How could a black person teach the language of Grisham and Waller? It was like letting a Ukrainian teach Polish. What *kind* of English would she be teaching? Would they land in New York and be taken prisoner by Harlem gangs?

Yeah, she'd say, that's a good one.

Can you imagine, she told Lander that evening, they take one look at me and sign up with some Australian dropout instead. Some Canadian. Some slushy-mouthed southerner. Some *Indian*. Weird vowels. Wrong rhythms. Serves them right.

The ham was small and fatty ('Good Polish ham is exported to Germany,' Slava apologized); she sliced it in strips and stuffed them inside *pyeroguies*. She was the cook. Rachel had always avoided the kitchen. They were a natural couple, speaking Polish and sometimes Russian or French. When Rachel was growing up, Lander had dreamed of sophistication for himself and his family, of an easy familiarity with the currents of the world, its languages. Strange that he should be the one adrift in itineraries and official meetings, scratching the surface of the earth. His daughter had accomplished it all on her terms, the world was no more complicated to her than the contingency of her passions. It seemed to him at the moment that nothing could be more appealing than coming home to a cheaply decorated colourful apartment in a seaside Polish resort and listening to Polish music on a kitchen portable in the company of two women stranger and more intimate to him than any two people in the world.

'We may emigrate to Australia,' she said. 'They recognize gay marriage.'

'When I was growing up, Australia was the ultimate white man's country,' he said. 'Bad as we were, we could pride ourselves at least we weren't South Africa and we weren't Australia.'

'Now, just look,' said his daughter. Slava was spooning out gobs of whipped cream over a rhubarb compote. 'Many Polish people are applying for South Africa, too.' The rhubarb colour matched the walls.

'Daddy,' she announced, 'we have a favour to ask.'

'Anything,' he said, regretting it immediately.

'It's big. You'll have to think about it.'

'Big brain,' he said. 'Big thought capability.'

'It's about Germany.'

'I've forgiven them. The Baltic is very forgiving.'

'They have a policy of return for Jews.'

'A little late. I'm happy where I am.'

'It's too late for you. Didn't we have property in Berlin?'

'*We*?'

Slava went back to the kitchen to throw handfuls of coffee into a pot of boiling water. She stayed longer than necessary.

'Didn't that psychiatrist uncle of yours have an office?'

'Uncle Henryk Sternfeld? He was Polish, but he had offices in Berlin. And Vienna.'

'Forget Vienna. Did he own it?'

Slava returned with coffee, and a plate of Swedish cookies.

'He might have. He was very successful. It would have been like him to own his office just to show that a Polish Jew could buy up a bit of Germany and analyse German patients. Of course, he would have gotten pleasure by renting it and taking their money and not investing in Germany at all.'

Slava turned to Tewfiqa. 'You say *gotten*? It sounds funny.'

'He would have *got* pleasure,' said Lander. 'He would especially have got pleasure owning a bit of Vienna. On Berggasse, near Freud. What are you driving at?'

'You're still my friend, Daddy? You'll still do anything?'

'I'm Daddy. Friend is a subset of Daddy.'

And then came the favour. The German government would restore ownership of private property to the survivor families of Jews uprooted – ('You mean rooted,' said Lander) – by the Nazis. The Poles would do the same for bourgeois families uncompensated by Communist seizures of property. Unfortunately, the Sternfelds had all been killed, but for Lander's mother, by the time the Communists took over. That left only Germany.

'Here is a copy of the deed, Dr Lander,' said Slava, in a mixture of German, which he understood, and French, which he found elusive. 'You see, we have done research. It is in the East Zone, near the main synagogue. Near Prenzlauerstraße, with all the whores and artists. A third-floor flat. Three rooms, high ceilings, balcony overlooking enclosed courtyard. Very nice. It can be yours.'

'It can be ours, Daddy,' said Tewfiqa.

Ours? he thought. *Ours*? In the name of all history, what exactly did 'ours' mean? The words slipped out like a grunt, as though he'd been kicked or slapped. *No* way. 'You want Great-uncle Henryk's old place? I can't.' *Don't be foolish*, he wanted to add. Have you no shame? Does history mean nothing to you? How can you even think such a thing? It was shocking, a chutzpah-update for the nineties. He thanked them for the dinner. He wished them luck with Australia.

As he was leaving, his daughter said, 'You have always been very fair to me. You gave me a good education. I played along with everything you wanted me to do.'

'And I hope to continue,' said Lander.

'But you never told me you love me. The only person who ever loved me was my mama, and I never even saw her.'

'I love you, Tewfiqa,' said Slava.

'We all love in our different ways,' said Lander. *Look at your fingers, for God's sake, she took your fingers, the spots on your ears, she abandoned you in a Dumpster!*

And then he walked out of his daughter's life. Lander had loved his mother, who'd taken Rachel on her lap in their dry-cleaner's shop, who'd wheeled her stroller in the park and said to the dubious and inquisitive, 'Isn't she smart?' It was in witnessing his mother's final Alzheimer's years that he'd developed his theories of the mind and language, the retention of personality, of humanity, despite appearances. Everything he stood for, in a way, was a monument to her.

Now it was in her name that the Germans were empowering him to act. History in its clumsy circuit had turned a brief spotlight on him. Is this what history had in mind? Restitution to adopted daughters? To *this* daughter, who makes a mockery of blood? Germany's blood myth admitted to citizenship any refugee with German blood, any displaced Volga or Paraguayan Mueller, any Vladimir or Carlos Schmidt, but denied it to Turks born and raised in their country. Is entitlement carried through blood alone? What would it do with Amber-Rachel-Tewfiqa Lander-Shvartz-Niggadyke?

No, he thought, it's absurd, a betrayal. History should die completely, his family should disappear entirely from this wretched continent, rather than give their killers the comfort of a generous apology. He wanted to keep faith with something clean and pure, a sharp break, not this salt-pillar of regret, this what-if, this second chance.

Lander strolled down the darkened, downward-sloping main street of Sopot towards the long, lighted wooden pier jutting into the Baltic, to the station to catch the last train into Gdansk. Gangs of young men in leather jackets, punk hair and chains shouted insults at him, made gestures, followed him a few feet cursing him in German. Some nights the thought of a good beating, at least a good fight, seemed restorative, an arbitrary end to rumination. A beer bottle was thrown, wide of the mark.

In the station, he waited with groups of teenagers, picnickers with water bottles and guitars, for the last train into Gdansk. It was Sunday night, their fair skins, the complexions of Ingeborg Holm and Hans Hansen, were pink from the sun. They sang, they joked, they'd be at work in the morning, bank clerks and salesmen and students, their peaceful bourgeois lives resumed after sixty years. No one knew him or noticed him. Maybe he seemed just Polish, which in a sense, he was.

His mother would put Rachel on her lap and allow her to punch the numbers on the customers' tickets. His mother pushed the stroller. 'What are you looking at? She's my granddaughter,' she'd say. 'Isn't she smart?' Loyalty to the greatness of his mother, that was the reason he was on this tour, why he could eat pyeroguies in his daughter's and her lover's rhubarb kitchen. It would be a hard case to make, the rich absurdity. The Germans won't get it. Do you apologize only to blood?

This is my daughter, isn't she smart? Her great-great-uncle was Henryk Sternfeld. Send the papers to my office.

A truth had been rising: When you meddle in fate for even the best of reasons, you force a realignment that implicates the universe. When the whole world screws you up, it takes even more of the world's resources to straighten you out. Rachel's case was dramatic, but so had Judy's been in the final years of their marriage, with her law degree, her suburban divorce-and-abuse practice, the repressed-memory cases, her conviction that the world she'd known had been a lie, that it was an evil and sinister place full of molesters, husbands and abusive mothers' boyfriends. The world had turned monstrous. She'd gone through madness before coming out the other end.

He'd been spared. His mother had saved him, his training had saved him, his professors, his colleagues. He'd clothed himself in virtue, like his great-uncle Henryk, seeing patients, listening to Mozart, until the border, all the borders, were sealed. The train arrived. Who knows, given a different history, he'd be a Polish psychiatrist like Uncle Henryk, going back to work in Gdansk from a weekend outing in the countryside. He had the face for it, the ancestry. He was one of the few men he'd ever met who could say after fifty years I'm leading the life I always wanted, I'm doing what I always intended, and what I have prepared myself for single-mindedly, still free to discover who I am and what I am capable of, and I'm not displeased. Is that not the modern definition of a monster?

White Children

I WAS BORN IN BROOKLYN in 1936. My earliest memory must be of the invasion of Poland, with my mother and our whole building screaming when they heard the names of bombed-out cities and overrun villages. Probably it left an impression because I was frightened for my own safety from bombs and Nazis in our own little extended Polish village off Flatbush Avenue. Adrenalin is a powerful memory-fixative.

I have vivid memories of Pearl Harbor Sunday, of FDR's death, and the dropping of the atomic bomb. Growing up, I saw all the war movies, especially the Pacific ones. In the fifties we made fun of cheap, copycat Japanese products. The Japanese could handle repetitive tasks competently enough, we were told, but we needn't fear their creativity. 'Usa' was a factory-city in central Japan created so they could stamp 'Made in USA' on the back of their flimsy tin toys held together with half-bent metal tabs. I was a twenty-seven-year-old assistant professor holding a white rat in the basement of the old lab on 166th Street with Kenji Wakamatsu, a postdoc fellow – I injecting a protein in the rat's brain and Kenji preparing to administer a shock – when a technician ran in shouting that Kennedy had been shot. It was Kenji who broke down and cried. We didn't think they did that.

Now I'm the visitor to Kenji's lab at Tokyo Neurolinguistic, and he's arranged a small apartment for me in a university-owned building across from Kanishikawa Park. Everything is miniaturized: The television, the refrigerator, the stove; the ceilings are low, the tables graze the rug, my knees come up to my shoulders when I sit on the sofa, and my sleeping mattress is on the floor. I can't cook or store more than one meal ahead; half a watermelon would engulf the kitchen. It's perfect for the *bonsai* life I lead. A friend once described the absurdity of his parents' lives, slow-moving and growing witless, brutalized by an oversized house, unable to get to a ringing phone in time, bullied by the family range (*cook, cook!*), the cavernous refrigerator (*cram, cram!*). The sheer dimension and convenience of their house had become an intimate bully. If only space could grow smaller, to match our disappearing mass in the universe and the fleeting time remaining to us.

I'm here, really, beyond the research and my friendship with Kenji and atonement for my ancient bigotries, to see my son, the Buddhist monk.

Meditating on ice last winter, Sammy froze four toes and had to have them amputated. Kenji told me to come quickly, we would try to save him. What kind of father allows his son to starve in robes and walk with a limp? My daughter is now a Polish lesbian, my ex-wife a recovered pill-addict. Sammy's former girlfriend, an Australian named Melanie, my potential daughter-in-law, mother of my fantasy grandchildren, told me he'd surrendered his toes graciously, even ecstatically. The monastery, according to Kenji, is known for its piety. Its monks hobble proudly, like lepers, on a fraction of their digits. They do not encourage visitors. To meet his fleshy father, his coincidental progenitor, to be reminded of a specific bodyshell, they say, would disrupt his meditation. And so I spend my days in Tokyo doing research in Kenji's lab, waiting for my son's *sensei* to give his permission for me to board the Bullet, then a bus, then to walk up the mountains to the monastery.

My daughter smokes. Of all the incongruities in my life, advice ignored, examples set, I sometimes think that's the most inexplicable of all.

In the post-dawn jogging cool-down every morning when I'm making my way back through Kanishikawa Park, I have to cut like a halfback through rows of old folks, mostly women, trudging silently to the park to do their exercises to piped-in music and recorded commands. They crouch like imaginary archers pulling back invisible strings. I am the youngest person among hundreds. Some mornings, it seems like quintessential warfare between mythical antagonists, my sweaty, against-the-current, personal exertion versus their flowing-downstream collective choreography. They stare at me, some mutter to their friends. I don't think they're saying, 'Look at this marvel of human engineering.'

In the park at five o'clock every afternoon an old man in khaki shorts and a Colorado Rockies baseball cap plays – without mood or inflection, and with recurrent flaws – one stanza of 'Stardust' on a dented trumpet. Men normally avoid exposing the sour slide of their fallibility in public (I've spent most of my fifty-nine years hiding even a hint); his tactless insouciance seems to me – perhaps I'm being sentimental – Japanese loneliness, the other side of so much community and public virtue.

We used to believe (and guys like me taught it) that you can never start training your children too early for a happy, productive life. By the age of two or three, they're already intact genetic and psychological entities. Nothing but a few social nuances can be added or subtracted. And so we read to our little entities, Rachel and Sam, we took them to plays and gallery openings, political rallies and poetry readings. We wanted them to share our irony and our passion, and all the discomforts of consciousness in a contingent universe. We wanted them to be stronger than we had been and to resist what we'd surrendered to. And of course, we wanted to be admired for all of it. We were the kind of parents any normal person despises.

(Now, when I hear young children coughing or crying at a concert, at a lecture or in a theatre, I want to shout: *If you can afford these prices, you can damn well afford a babysitter!* Spare me conversation during the opening credits of a movie, don't even ruin the Coke and popcorn ads, the trailers, don't destroy the atmosphere of surrender).

I remember those lecturers and their rhetorical questions from the podium: *Is this thing working?* (how I copied all their mannerisms! I knew I'd be a featured lecturer one day and that the witty, casually informative introductions I was labouring over would someday be another assistant professor's rehearsed ad-libs for me; great halls would fill, *for me*, and I'd have to practise the proper modest attitude, the solicitous concern for acoustics): *How about the back, can you hear me?* And Sam, who was four, would shout back, *I can hear you, Mister Beard!* Such a bright, confident, unselfconscious little guy, people would say. Once, at a great poet's last public reading, Sam started crying. I thought he'd developed a tummyache. *He's so sad*, little Sam explained. Such a kind, empathetic, tenderhearted child, well ahead of the pace of Piaget's theories. We were raising a genius of compassion and we didn't know how to deal with it.

This little boy of ours was an unfailing delight. Judy had had three miscarriages, then we'd adopted Rachel and she was a chore to manage, to bring back to life. She'd been abandoned in a Harlem Dumpster, she'd lost a finger, part of her ears, she had congenital heroin dependency. Then Sam, the miracle child, and uneventful pregnancy, and easy delivery – anxious to please even as a baby. Son-challenged at the *seder*, he was always our wise son, sometimes our simple son; Rachel always played the wicked child.

I loved him without limit or reservation. I woke him up if I came home late, I put him on my shoulders when we shopped. I ran up and down the aisles, along the sidewalks, down the office hallways, and he giggled (he had that easy laugh that I'd never mastered – my father would have discouraged it anyway); I held him in my lap, nibbled on his precious ears, blew on his neck, caressed that babysoft hair, God! that new baby smell, like a puppy or a kitten that we didn't want to have grow up too fast, but he stayed adorable at every age. I thrilled to his perfect little body running, always running, through the apartment. I wanted him running, eternally. I wanted to be his protector, forever.

And now he limps, walks with a stick. His ribs show, I'm told, though I'm not allowed to see him. His balding scalp is shaved. They've taken away his glasses.

He responded with love. He loved strangers, he was never shy, he trusted everyone and everything, a babysitter's delight. When bedtime came he'd sneak down the hall to his room, trailing his blanket, blowing a kiss and saying only, '*Me go pleep now*,' without our having to settle him down. Rachel, we practically had to dope, to tie down, to visit a dozen times in the night.

Sam rewrote all the manuals: No teething problems, no Terrible Twos, no jealousy, no selfishness. *Me go pleep now* still makes me smile, sometimes cry. He brought out the best in everyone, even his sister. She'd push his carriage, change him, answer back to Blacks in the park who'd demand an explanation for a little black girl attending a white boy.

'He's my brother, you fool!' I never loved her more. She called him Sam Lander the Salamander, not unkindly. She still calls him Sal.

I'm at a loss. He was untroubled and precocious. People used to say when he was eight years old, that little boy has *soul.* I can't believe that it's just my ego insisting that I'm somehow at the centre of everything, somehow to blame. I must have done something shattering. How did I let him down? I can't remember. He's lost, I can't find him, he's what my father called *a minyan in Minot*, a needle in a haystack. Rachel blames me for everything in her life, as did Judy, so I feel entitled to claim just a little responsibility for his russet robes, his mutilated feet and his ribs sticking out. I think back to that perfect little body running down our narrow hallway. I wait for 'Stardust', and I cry.

When Sam was nine or ten, he would go into Manhattan with me on the train and head to the museums with just a sketchbook and pencils. We didn't worry about security in those days. What could be safer for a boy than a day in the museum with a sketchpad, then joining his father for lunch? It was a delight to sit with such an attentive little boy who couldn't wait to get back to the Natural History or the New York State Museum in order to sit in front of the cases and sketch. He had that omnivorous attention to the world that all bright children have at some time, before age and education dim it, the ability to rattle off facts learned from plaques about Indian encampments, mastodon hunts, old subway cars, reconstructed interiors of immigrant tenements.

He was good at all of it, his drawings plastered my office doors and corkboards. I remember the diorama of *Cold Water Flat, Brooklyn, 1889,* from the New York City Historical Museum. 'That's the way we lived,' I told him, 'your great-grandparents lived just like this.' Even in the Brooklyn of my childhood, I'd lived six or seven years like that, those first memories of Poland and Pearl Harbor came from bathing in the kitchen sink and looking out the window onto the street, and I remembered the clothes hanging out the back, the ice-deliveries, the shouts and crying from other apartments sharing our airshaft, and I'd quickly add happy stories of my mother heating the water on the gas rings for my bath in the kitchen sink, the cut-rate Elijahs rented from large families who timed their doorknocking to add drama to the *seder*. Otherwise, even the poverty of my childhood made him sad. I'd take him through the labs to the faculty lunchroom and introduce him to my colleagues.

Kenji remembered him, when he was two. In a roundabout way it's the reason I was invited to Tokyo Neurolinguistic, thirty years later. Sam called on Kenji when he came to Tokyo just three years ago. Back then, Sam was a different sort of person, worldly and fun-loving, looking up my friends, taking strangeness in stride.

After college Sam left to see the world and to learn off-beat languages, for which he had a knack. Two years stretched to seven. He became a D.J. in Thailand, started English schools in Korea and Indonesia, and finally landed an advertising job among lively expats in Tokyo. He had an apartment in Roppongi, he learned Japanese, he had Japanese girlfriends, then Melanie, and then everything stopped. No letters, no calls, mail returned. Now, Melanie says, he's lost sixty pounds and he looks like Woody Allen playing Yul Brynner.

I worried that we'd deprived him of a normal childhood, the very reason we'd moved out to Chappaqua. No Little League, no Scouts, no music lessons or summer camps – that was Rachel's business, at which she excelled. He didn't want to give up his precious summers with me and the museums in the city. Neither did I.

Did I set him up to become a Buddhist when we took him to Australia for a year, putting the kids in an Adelaide suburban junior high? Australia to me was just another lab with friendly colleagues and a chance to interview Aborigines and study their language acquisition, aging and language loss, a pleasant house on a river where kids trapped platypuses, and kangaroos nibbled the hedges, but a city and country, for Judy and me, of no great consequence. But for Sam and Rachel, Australia was a full new society, a city to explore, new sports to learn, a set of new models and standards, where their accents set them apart. Six months in a strange place when you're an adolescent, compared to ten years when you're an adult, and the consequences are like a meteor slamming to earth instead of a light spring shower. He came back from Australia sounding like a perfect Oz, knowing the cricket and rugby stars, the local music. Perhaps settling down even in that most American of countries doomed my children to lives of permanent exile. Not just exile; transformation.

In Tokyo, I've learned to turn abstinence into a kind of hedonism. It pleases me to shop at the neighbourhood Co-op like an elderly pensioner, to weigh out spotty apples and woody carrots, to select a dehydrated dinner from well-stocked shelves. Every selection is a total surprise, no English on any package, no instructions I can follow, no taste I can expect. Sweet or salty, meat or fruit, I won't know till I take a bite. Clear plastic bottles filled with liquid; shampoo or cooking oil? I don't know the language, but I feel I can read the faces, the body language. It's reassuring to be surrounded by elaborate signs, knowing none of them apply to me. The opposite of Alzheimer's must be Kafka's disease, where everything points to you, but lacks all meaning. The steak house at the top of the street features a two-hundred-dollar dinner of *matsuzaka* beef, not just prime Kobe, but eating in Tokyo for under two dollars – that's adventure. Tokyo has rendered me slightly Alzheimered, unable to read, to respond, to learn from context. I've become an abstinence junkie.

I wonder if Sam went through any of this. He always had a native woman with him, he mastered languages from local dialects, he learned to cook the local cuisine. He knew the most specialized words, things a professor would have to look up, because he started with the fruits and vegetables, birds and trees, the cuts of meat, the fish, the sexual moves, the grammar of seamless belonging.

I like to think I have an appreciation for mysticism. In other centuries, science and mysticism were not so far apart. Then, ten years ago, quite literally, I dreamed my future. Faces started entering my dreams, my brain went on a kind of untethered voyage. At first, the faces frightened me, like circulating malignancies looking for a host organ. Other nights I would rush to bed, monitoring diverse populations trying to escape my brain, or gain admission. My brain was just a mediator between past and future.

(Now, I spend my nights in guilty dreams. I seem to have crossed wires with remorseless villains. Murderer! Liar! Disfigurer! The first hour of every morning is a long waking from nighttime dread.

Thank God it was only a dream! But I used to trust my dreams, they contained visions and good advice.)

Ten years ago, I said yes to a challenge, or what I interpreted as a challenge. I was married, the children were grown. I'd served on the school board, done my bit for Democrats when even old friends were turning Reaganite, pushed for recycling and better race relations. I had a lawn to manage, dogs to walk, tickets to sports and cultural events, cars in the driveway, parties to give and to go to. I had a mother, failing in her mind, to visit. At times, like everyone, I felt like an unclaimed suitcase going round and round on a baggage carousel. Mislabelled? Abandoned? My face and body had begun to sag, like an underpacked, soft-sided suitcase after a long trip, revealing the outlines of something vague and resistant inside. I didn't know it was a bomb. I looked into the mirror and thought: It's not so bad today, but I don't want this process to go any further. Standard midlife crisis stuff. All in all, a good life, proper for a man turning fifty.

If an informed choice had been offered (maybe it's never a choice, more a Bargain with the Cosmic Prompter) to persist in the comforting life of exercise bikes, educational and slightly risky vacations (Cuba, Egypt, China, South Africa), fruit-tree pruning and dog breeding, investment tracking, harmless flirtations, or something more dangerous: surrendering to your dreams – literally, entering the landscape of your nightly release – exploring the power of your brain's own programming (is it Microsoft that asks, 'Where do you want to go today?' My advice is, unplug, don't answer), I would never have picked up the option. I would have stayed in Chappaqua.

By yielding to the challenge, I set in motion a series of events that implicated the world. I was given access to a population inside my head. It was a mystic's vision – that I might just be a drop of blood in the universe, but that drop was a diagnostic motherlode containing the whole world, everything ever written or known, every life ever lived, every landscape ever explored – but I was a scientist and it's very inconvenient for a scientist to receive such a prompt. Better to treat it as a symptom of something repressed. Buy a red Miata, have an affair, stay in Chappaqua.

Somehow, like a child picking berries who sees a bat flying from the hillside, or who feels a rush of cold air from a cleft in the rocks, I had stumbled into a fissure. But that fissure was in my head, a pathway of hyper-speech that should have been closed by normal speech, by social training, by the protocols of science itself. Those faces, those dreams, were the bats pouring from the hillside, and I entered (or it entered me, I was asleep), and I found inside my skull a lightless crystal palace, prehistoric bones, lampblack sketches, colourless fish and the agency of bats. A harder, more contingent universe than I ever suspected. The brain's software is infinite, Master Bill. I have been living in that cave for the past ten years.

I remember a moment from Erasmus Hall, my dear old school in Brooklyn, when the majesty of algebra dawned in my life, its appropriateness to every thought in the universe. I know that waking dream of my fourteen-year-old self as a precursor to nighttime dreams of fifty; I know that everything in my life between fifteen and fifty was, essentially, a diversion from truth. I heard music that day, the room went dark purple, the other students disappeared. The beauty of the numbers was overwhelming, like the night sky in the planetarium. Everything in the world can be made equal to something else! There's a formula to balance everything! The universe is composed of equivalents! The world is a balance of push and pull, light and dark, action and reaction. Every single term, every figure, every expression, can be balanced by something else. It seemed more powerful than antibiotics; algebra was a kind of purely mental penicillin. That's what all the great minds were doing: Applying algebra, finding the equation for neutralizing evil or suffering or poverty. I say *this* equals *that* because I've put an equal sign between them; all I have to do now is solve the equation for *x*.

Is that what made him a Buddhist monk, Sam's equivalent *satori*, an early attachment to staged interiors, to the presumed purity of the diorama, to looming silent forms permanently caught with spears in their hands against a staggering mastodon, their women permanently pounding meal and flax, that, and discovering a cache of platypus eggs and accidentally destroying them from too much love, the taunts of a black sister and crying over Holocaust poetry at the age of four?

2.

'You cod-sperm jockeys are all alike,' says Kenji in mock anger. 'Yesterday *shirako* was on the menu. Today it's out of season.' We're on our weekly pub-crawl and restaurant-binge. He writes out *shirako* – cod sperm – for me in Chinese characters: 'white' / 'children'. I spend the week on ramen noodles and dried dinners, proud of a perverse penury that takes me through Tokyo on five dollars a day. I break free on Friday nights. I've been in Tokyo for the night of luminous dwarf squid, when the plates are served in the dark and you can follow the twinkling lights of a hundred chopsticks. I've eaten my way through sardine runs and the spawning of transparent shrimp. I've consumed the guts and brains and eyes of everything that sinks or swims or floats in Japanese water. In the place of cod-sperm he whips up a plate of salted squid gut.

'You want it fresh, don't you?' leers the *sashimi* chef as he carves bouquets, like unfolding roses, of beet-red tuna. 'Just like the lady cod. She likes her *shirako* real fresh.'

'*Seku hara*, too!' I interject, and the chef throws up his hands. How Japanese, to have learned the word for sexual harassment in a sashimi bar. It doesn't matter where I pick up words, contexts don't count. At nearly sixty, I'm a two-year-old in Japanese, grabbing at fleeting objects, unable to read or to express my needs and ideas. Thank God for baseball, a familiar, transferable attachment; thank God for sumo, something new to appreciate. Thank God for the beautiful logic of Japanese.

If I were a small, polite man in a black business suit, mindful of every step I took, observing the painful intricacies of a ritualized society, I too would dream sumo dreams, buffing up to a quarter ton, stripping down to an orange breechclout, planting one foot on Honshu, another on Kyushu, and gut-butting an opponent all the way to Okinawa.

'Sumo – lose it, or use it!' Kenji had joked. He led me through the tournament. Sumo stables like baseball clubs, colours like racing silks.

Maybe once a week I get the urge for company and restaurant food, and I call Kenji. Hence the cod-sperm bars with televised baseball, the salted squid guts, the weekly trip to our favourite *yakitoria* at Yurukucho, tucked among the girders under the Hibiya El. Waiters rush from table to table taking orders by cellphone in the smoky gloom. There was a time when languages fired my brain, like walking in an unfamiliar city long enough to gain comfort, make friends, find love. The years are gone when I could do a city on my own, when the streets and monuments, the smattering of new words, the growing familiarity that comes with a week of walking, taking subways and buses, when the magnificence of alien anonymity is enough to satisfy me. I need Kenji.

Kenji Wakamatsu and I are the same age, although I think of him as younger. He's trim and dark-haired (although he dyes it); I'm plump despite the running. I think of the matted grey hairs on the top of my head as a personal web-site. He'd been my student and he'd already published more than I had but he'd needed American certification for possible immigration purposes, and so he had placed himself in my class. A college teacher, I'd decided in shame, should be older than his students, wiser if not smarter, and more published. Kenji's presence helped me retire from teaching and to stay in research.

'If you could train your crows to eat cigarette butts, Tokyo would be the cleanest city in the world,' I tell him. We're walking at night along my morning running route, avoiding the restaurants I know by the fragrance of their overnight garbage. He's looking for a *mukokuseki* restaurant, something new to show me from Tokyo's 'bubble' days in the eighties when Japan felt it could afford to take the best from the rest of the world, mix them up, Korean and French, Mexican and Chinese, Italian and Thai, with a Japanese spin.

Without Kenji, Tokyo would be a meaningless maze. He tells me I did the same for him in those New York years, but I can't remember walks we took, or meals, only lists of suggested readings. He remembers baseball games, and where else could he have learned the Dodger lineups of the fifties, Yankee games of the sixties, except from me? He swears we watched Mantle and Maris together; now we watch Mitsui, the young stud of the Yomiuri Giants, and the six-hundred-pounders of Sumo. He remembers my mother, meals I took him to in Brooklyn. Perhaps Kenji's New York was like Sam's Adelaide, a time of accelerated growth that left him forever dissatisfied with Japan and exquisitely tuned to America. He travels as much I do, we move over the surface of the world like touring pros, hitting the opens, shmoozing with the sponsors.

'Try the *patapata-gyoza*.' he suggests, and I check the English menu: *meat-stuffed boned chicken wings*. Other entrees seem jauntily existential: 'Let's roll wild duck meat and vegetables together by lettuce and see what happens!' He takes the squid and corn lasagna.

'Boned and deboned mean the same thing, don't they?' he asks. 'What's a foreigner to do?'

'Gutted and degutted. Seeded and seedless.'

'It suggests a certain deft but elusive logic,' he says. 'What is empty? Is it empty, or is it air-stuffed?'

'Sammy used to say I had a lot of baldness.'

'*Going to bat for someone* – means standing up for him, no? But if you literally go to bat for someone, you are removing him from the game, right?'

'How about recover?' I say. 'It should mean re-burial, but it means to restore. How can you recover and still get out of bed?'

'We're in trouble, my friend. Japanese, on the other hand, is so logical. Think of the white children.'

'*Second to none*. Supposed to be a compliment – think about it.'

'We get less Alzheimer's, too,' he said.

In his spare time, drawing on his American years, Kenji translates American writers, from self-help books to serious novels. If he had not been a Japanese male of his generation with parents and a family to support and a society to rebuild, he would have been a writer. He feels it his personal mission to rid Japanese culture of its mysterious anti-Semitism. It must not be easy, translating Dr Ruth and Cynthia Ozick, among others, into Japanese.

'I'm a child of the restaurant business,' he'd confided to me on other evenings, if only to apologize for certain pedantic asides that I always found fascinating. But this evening I want to talk of Sam; Kenji's culinary history doesn't seem appropriate. I fear that his monastery will be forever closed to me, that he's suffering and I will never see him. Kenji has been handling my petitions.

'This society calls itself Confucian, but we inherited Confucianism from China,' he says. 'Getting imported concepts slightly wrong is our saving national virtue, I feel. What you're up against is monks who think they are very good Confucianists and very good Zen Buddhists. They can therefore be hard and inflexible, then just as suddenly, enigmatic and compliant.'

'I'm waiting for some flexibility.'

'Unfortunately, they have no concept of waiting.'

And then he lights a cigarette, leans back, and smiles at me. Another chapter in the bright book of Japanese life, Kenji's personal history, is about to unfold. 'This is, in a way, about waiting,' he says. 'Your grandfather came to New York from –'

'Riga,' I say.

'Yes, beautiful Riga. Well, Riga in a sense came to my grandfather. It was 1884. He was five years old, and so far as he ever knew, an orphan. That is, he remembers no life before the arrival of Germans in Edo harbour. He remembers speaking no language but German, no food, no clothes, but German. A German boat came to Edo to establish a German embassy, and he eventually became a German cook. He never learned to cook Japanese. Even his wife was only a German cook. Pork, sauerkraut, sausages, beer, white wine. He learned to make all of it.

'Their son, my father, learned the art of German cooking inside the embassy. When they became our enemy in the First War, my grandfather quit and started a German restaurant. Even during the war, German officers used to eat at the Goldenes Adler.

'Between the wars, it was the most popular restaurant in Tokyo. My first memories are of peeling potatoes in the back of the restaurant. I think we'd already bombed Pearl Harbor – sorry, my friend. It was an exciting time to be Japanese. A wonderful time! You can't imagine the entertainers we had, the German singers, the Chinese acrobats, the slave labour from Korea and the Philippines! Oh, the artwork from Bali, the birds from New Guinea! My father was a young man, and feeling very imperial. We had an unlimited food supply from all the countries we'd conquered. The clientele were all diplomats and navy brass and their girlfriends. We were the very centre of Tokyo society. The whole German Asian fleet ate at our restaurant every night. My father decorated the place in swastikas.

'And then, you can guess. The fortunes of war started turning. We lost the lands, we lost the trade, and gradually we lost the diplomats and the admirals. We couldn't get fresh meat or vegetables and the commercial fishing boats were taken over by the navy to camouflage their equipment against air attacks.

'I remember every night running a thick black line through another menu item. *Unavailable.* Finally, there was nothing left, not fish soup, not even German beer. He refused to serve *miso* soup, and even our Korean help offered to make *kimchi*, but he would not serve anything Asian, because he was a German chef and we were a German restaurant. Then the American firebombing came and wiped out our house and killed my brother.'

"*Thirty Seconds Over Tokyo,*" I said. 'I remember it well.' Even fondly.

'A week after the fire, my father went to the restaurant, took out a boning knife, or was it a deboning knife, wrapped himself in the German flag and committed *seppuku* in the kitchen. I was nine or so, and I had to extract the blade. It was a small blade, he did not perform the ritual as he should have. He was not sufficiently Japanese, consequently he must have died in agony over many, many hours. You see, *Wurst* and *Schnitzel* and *Kartoffelsalat* were the only things he knew. He had this fierce, inflexible dedication. He had an almost inherited sense of honour, but nothing to apply it to. He was fulfilling a destiny. I think of him as prototypical of my culture, at its most vulnerable. Personally, I'd always wished my grandfather had at least been picked up by a French boat.'

'It's a great novel, Kenji. It's a beautiful film. But is it about waiting?'

'It's about not-waiting,' he smiled. 'A deft and illusive form of waiting, and a little bit about getting foreign messages just a little wrong.' He twirled a bit of squid lasagna on his fork. 'No one should die over sauerkraut,' he said.

3.

Melanie is dark-haired and tending to flesh. She seems Mediterranean, though her last name is Scottish. She came to Tokyo to temp in an English-language office and gradually drifted to English duties in a Japanese business. She'd met Sam at an Australian party; he'd arrived with a Japanese girl and left with her. They just hit it off, she said. She'd never met anyone with his spirituality.

The first time she visited me, she dropped off pictures of Sammy, the Sammy I knew, smiling, a little fleshy himself. Melanie in those pictures was slender, and quite the beauty. I gathered from her use of the past tense that she did not expect to see him again.

When I opened the door the first time, early in my Tokyo stay, her greeting went: 'Hello, Dr Lander, I believe we've met before.'

I thought, as I always do, yes, of course, analogically speaking, we've met. My son, our mutual loss, our near father-daughter relationship. 'I feel like we have,' I said.

'Many times,' she pushed.

I frowned, affably. 'Many letters, many calls, indeed.'

'Many billions, perhaps trillions of times,' she said, but tossing it off with a giggle. This, I thought, was excessive, even on the molecular level. Easy profundity; it happens to westerners in Asia. 'I've been in this room many billions of times,' she said, patting the low table, 'Do you know how many times Japan has risen from the sea?'

'I'm afraid I don't.'

'Never mind. The Enlightened Ones know. Sam knows. Sam is spiritually awake.'

When she says spiritually, she doesn't mean it lightly. She means incense and vegetarianism, aligning her foods and mattress and who knows what with heavenly and earthly forces, invisible to us but known to the ancients, to devotees, to the awakened. She leads her life under a spell of taboos which she calls mantras of freedom.

That first Sunday she took me out to Harajuko, where, she said, she and her friends were performing. She wasn't dressed for performance unless she was in a Shaker band.

On the subway, we talked. She had taken the subway a trillion-trillion times. We'd had this conversation an infinite number of times, of course – didn't I remember any of it?

Sammy was beginning to remember his past lives, she said. We had to get him away from all his distractions. The Enlightened One remembers a million lives, which is like, maybe, thirty seconds in a lifetime.

Are we talking about the Buddha? I finally asked.

The Buddha is an aspect of the Enlightened One. So is Christ, and the Prophet. Isn't it amazing how all the great men of vision are blind? They have the inner light.

Darwin? Freud? Ramanujan? I asked.

Aspects of the Enlightened One, she answered, smiling. Homer, Tiresias, Milton. Sheik Omar Rahman. And of course the Perfect Master. Her face made a slight contortion, ending in radiance.

Ray Charles? Stevie Wonder? I almost asked. I finally demanded to know, Who is this Perfect Master?

He has an earthly name for this transit, of course. He was born blind to human parents. But his name is the Enlightened One, she said.

And what constitutes his perfect wisdom? I asked.

Everything we see, everything we do or think has happened trillions of times before. We have had this very same conversation a trillion times before. Japan has risen from the oceans, man has evolved from germs and bacteria, someone has invented subways, America and Japan are destined to annihilate each other, all of this has happened and is happening and will happen again. It is not just astronomy that deals in big numbers, Dr Lander, it's little things like subway tickets and sex and children playing soccer in that field over there. Everything is déjà vu a million-million times. So everything we do or say has only a million-millionth of the importance we think it does.

Pardon my objection, but that is easy profundity, I said. But I was thinking, ... isn't this the stuff of poetry, too, Tennyson or was it Blake? ...*flower in the crannied wall*... I was thinking of my adolescent self in the world of equations. I could see Sammy standing in my place, on this subway, looking down on this plump, serene face and body, and suddenly I felt terror, I could see him taking the next step. I could see myself, not so many years ago, taking the same step.

You and I have had this misunderstanding before, she said, and we've settled it with sex before – yes, that too is ordained – I know we'll meet again but we may be billions of years older, so we won't know it.

Yes, I thought, sex had entered the dialogue. I quickly changed the subject. We're talking stellar collapse, is that it? The universe pulsing like a hummingbird's heart, in-out, two hundred beats a minute, each beat a forty-billion-year cycle? So nothing that happens in this heartbeat has any significance, no meaning should be attached to anything ... I shouldn't care about my son – is that it?

Sam would want you to be happy, she said.

Sexually?

In every way, like the other times.

A button had come undone. We were standing in a Tokyo subway, I was staring into cleavage and a warm zombie had just propositioned me.

She smiled. Geniuses in every discipline are given a vision of the unity of all things, don't you reckon, Dr Lander?

I said I reckoned they were.

The Enlightened One was given such a vision.

And what exactly is his vision?

We've risen from germs and bacteria to becoming me and you and Sammy a trillion-trillion times before. Japan has risen from the ocean and sunk below it a trillion-trillion times. America and Japan have destroyed each other trillions of times. Liberation comes from realizing that everything that will happen has already happened. But you see, he remembers a million transits, that is why he knows everything a million times better than the unawakened. You have written your books a trillion times and their tapes have been played to him at least a million times – that is why he is so interested in Sammy. You and Sammy have already joined us, in other transits. This time, we're going to break the cycle for everyone. The Enlightened One has secret plans.

Tell me about them.

Naughty, naughty, then they wouldn't be secret, would they? She clung to the pole in the middle of the subway car, a fetching pose. Sammy and me, we knew each other before, you know?

A trillion times, I'm sure, I said.

No, not that way! In *this* transit, in Adelaide. We were in school together in seventh grade! He was this American bloke. He remembered me, right off. Said he had a crush on me, can you imagine? Came to a party with a girl named Keiko, left with me. Fate, I'd call it.

He didn't have a chance, did he? I tried to smile.

I can remember twelve ... no, thirteen, other transits and Sammy never came to Adelaide in any of them. So the Enlightened One is right, this transit is different.

We came to the station, the crowd surged, I could barely keep up. Thousands of us filled the pedestrian skyways and off in the distance, lining a closed-off parkway were the parked vans and portable stages of at least fifty bands. Live music, as far as the eye could see. Tens of thousands of Sunday strollers walked through the woods, stopping at food kiosks.

It's not just old American ballplayers who go to Japan to die – so do the fifties, sixties, seventies and eighties. Each band specialized in a style, and the style was perfectly reproduced: Heavy metal, glitter, punk, grunge, country and western, classic rock 'n' roll. Kool Kizz, Loft, Vanity, Vanishing Point. There were Alice Cooper and David Bowie lookalikes, Elvis clones, Beach Boys and Beatles, even some religious cults in their Hawaiian shirts and white pants, whumping tambourines and smiling beatifically.

As I feared, Melanie was one of the tambourine girls behind a threesome of toothy, bleached blond boys lip-synching Christian lyrics to feather-light rock. I stood in the middle of the roadway as long as I could bear it, thinking: My Sammy, his love and credulity, all his empathy and sketching; he had found a different father. My son was dead, and I had killed him.

I wanted to get away, not from the Japanese imitators, not from the packs of stylized dancers twisting away to elaborate choreography in tight jeans, boots, and T-shirts, fifties greased rhino-heads with foot-high do's, with air-guitar, combswiping and breakdancing routines, unlit cigarettes dangling at James Dean angles, the Marlboro packs twisted in the T-shirts over the tattooed biceps, the practised Elvis snarl; it was the sweet harmonies, the fake-Hawaiian hipswaying invitation to come inside, take the literature, meet the counsellors. It was Melanie, whacking a tambourine high over her head, a third my age from the land down under who represented that day the face of an evil I thought had vanished from my world.

4.

One morning, my subway train was halted and boarded. Policemen ordered us to abandon everything, and whisked us up staircase and emergency ladders to the street. No one complained, no one questioned. The procedure went calmly, as one might expect in a country where policemen wear white gloves. Just a few minutes later, we knew the reason. If I'd been on an earlier train, I might be dead. People on that train had been struck by a mysterious illness.

'Now you know. Our dirty little secret is out,' said Kenji that same evening. By most reckoning, it was the darkest night in modern Japanese history. Nothing had changed since the cult of emperor-worship, the bombing of Shanghai, the Japanese enslavement of the rest of Asia. Kenji had spent the day in tears. Modern Japan was a fraud, every bit of progress of the past fifty years had been wiped out. 'I warned you,' he said, 'we are an astonishingly crude country. We're all presentation.'

'Kenji, it's just a lone madman.'

Nothing had yet been announced, but Kenji had his suspicions. It was a religious cult led by a blind man. He didn't trust the telephone; we met in his favourite loud and smoky retro-future yakitoria, under the girders of Hibiya station. The country had already entered the trauma-zone. Everyone was looking over his shoulder for fear he was not seen denouncing it loudly and publicly enough – random killing of Japanese by Japanese – the fear that someone, in years to come, might sort through pictures of that evening and find a crease of merriment on anyone's face. It was Kabuki, the painted-on grimace. 'This is an evil greater than any we have know,' Kenji said. His hair was uncombed, white at its roots; I had never noticed the unruly, almost corrugated thickness of his eyebrows. 'It's home-grown pollution. It's the corruption of our collective soul.'

I wanted to touch him, to offer some measure of inclusion in the

American century. Welcome to the millennium. Men in the standard young executive 'salaryman' black suits and white shirts, like a convention of Jehovah's Witnesses, were crying. Nothing the Japanese could do, no crime, based on my four months' residency, placed them beneath the plunging standards of world behaviour. You're not innocents! I wanted to cry out, Shit happens! This isn't Sweden after Palme's assassination. But the Japanese persisted. The country had sinned, its elites had betrayed a misguided, materialist society. The same country that refused to apologize for wartime atrocities, that denied well-documented massacres of Asian civilian populations, had turned its arrogance inward.

'That's it,' said Kenji. 'We never accepted our wartime guilt. We took punishment without ever acknowledging guilt.'

Patterns were emerging. The blind leader, the blind enthusiasm, the religious appeal, the enrolment of foreigners in a Japanese cause. Sammy, unfortunately, would know about it.

I asked him about my son, this time for the whole truth.

'He's in Hokkaido. I keep writing.'

'I think you're trying to hide him. I think he's involved.'

He made a shushing sound, held a finger to lips. 'He had no involvement. Maybe a little prior knowledge. He wanted to escape, but they wouldn't let him.'

'I have to see him. Where is he?' I had visions of dark cellars, safe houses, jail cells, mental hospitals.

'He didn't want you to see him,' said Kenji. 'He wanted to regain his strength. I thought it would be a simple thing, bringing you here, getting him out –'

'– and then she showed up?'

'They were using her to get to you, to get to him.' Ah, the fatal button. 'They kill anyone who tries to leave. They have agents at the airports, in the visa offices, their computers tap into everything. If he showed up anywhere, they'd get to him. I call it protection, but I've been lying to you every day about your son.

'What do you know of the Ainu people?' he asked.

Back in my student days, some linguists and anthropologists thought the Ainu, animist, tattooed, hunter-gatherers, heavily bearded, bear-worshippers of Hokkaido, Sakhalin and the Kuriles, were the aboriginal Japanese. They appeared to be Caucasian, or at least, non-Asian in features. They had no written language, just a rich set of oral histories, mainly explaining how the natural world came to be.

'I thought they were extinct,' I said.

'All but a few hundred. They are a pure people,' he said. 'Their hearts are noble. When I was still in high school I volunteered to work with the Ainu for the summer, like an American going to an Indian reserve.'

We were off on another Kenji story, this time more urgently, and, I sensed, intimately involved with Sammy.

'They believe everything has a soul. Earth, sky, mountains, animals, fish. They live a very brutal life, but they are the most spiritual people in Japan. Before I die, the last pureblooded Ainu will probably also be gone.'

What I had learned of the Ainu came from linguists and anthropologists thirty-five years ago. Back then it was said the unwritten, nearly extinct Ainu language was possibly linked to the Altaic tongues of central Siberia, with their connections to Estonian and Finnish. Others said no, there were Malayo-Polynesian remnants in the speech, indicating a link to south Asia, New Guinea, Australia, and the Dravidians of India. Either the Ainu had worked their way eastward from Siberia, onto Sakhalin and down to Hokkaido, or northward from the Malay peninsula, through the Philippines, Okinawa, Kyushu and Honshu, pushed by wars and landgrabs all the way to coastal Hokkaido. Both possibilities were exciting to a young linguistics scholar in the early sixties, attempting to arrive at a universal linguistic paradigm. Ainu was one of those link languages, the people one of those inexplicable genotypes, an undeciphered Rosetta stone.

Nowadays, the romance is gone. The language has been judged an isolate, a kind of far-east Basque. The people appear to be related to the Australian Aborigines, and are not even especially ancient, or particularly pure. Over the millennia they'd intermarried with every Asian tribe in their path.

But all I said to Kenji was, 'The one thing I remember about the Ainu was a line in one of the early reference books. "Their women are exceptionally ugly.'" That passed for scholarship, a generation or two before our own.

'You'll have a chance to see for yourself,' he said.

Many years ago, when the Soviet Union was breaking up, I met a woman named Ainu, in Estonia. I joked about her name, the hairy, aboriginal people it called to mind, although the note on ugliness did not apply to her. Like most Estonians, she knew all about the Ainu. During the Russian occupation, Estonia might have been the *samizdat* Ainu research centre of the world. She was proud of her name. In those white summer nights she lectured me on Estonia's link to Japan. Estonians don't have European blood, literally; despite appearances, they are Asian. Their myths are not Greek or Roman, not of Nordic or Celtic gods; they have legends of a small, hairy, bear-worshipping people and of the struggle in the forests between dark bear-worshippers and the blond, invading hockey players we know today. Their blood and myths were absorbed.

In those years, the Estonians were desperate to find any link to any non-Russian, non-German past. Japan was the only world power not taken. A giant boulder in the east of Estonia had been proclaimed the oldest rock in the world, a space relic from the origins of the universe, perhaps even bearing the first molecules of life itself. Three weeks free of Russia and they were quietly forging the algebra of a new identity. Estonia, my temporary Ainu, was the link between space and earth, eternity and the present, speech, blood, myth, DNA, east and west, everything but the Garden of Eden, and on a molecular level, perhaps even that.

I thought suddenly, it all applied to Japan as well. Not so nakedly, not so plaintively, but far more dangerously.

'I received word from your son's *sensei*,' he said. 'It's good news. We can leave tomorrow.'

Much can be forgiven a society that invents and uses the Bullet train. Riding the Bullet brings back that pre-Interstate, pre-Jumbojet promise of magneto-trains that were going to take us from New York to Chicago in an hour, with stops. Not so much distance-travel as time-travel, geography as time-lapse photography. Tokyo peels away, the suburbs fall, jewelled gardens glitter like lacquered boxes, hundreds of kilometres pass and we're never out of sight of clustered houses and multi-storied buildings, with their city-block squares of rice paddies and tended orchards in between, vegetable patches, greenhouses, and more rice paddies carpet the flatlands, orchards bloom on hillsides, mountains rise, until giant pine forests block the sun. 'Look, a monastery up there,' Kenji would point out with delight, and I'd think, hopefully, *Sammy?* but, no, it was just the overlay of time and cultures, like castles on the Rhine, and Kenji gave no signs. Watching the landscape transform itself is like a vision of successive creations, this folding and smoothing of the Japanese islands, all the way to Sapporo. Thank God I'm an atheist.

For hours we skimmed the coast, past fishing villages untouched by this century. Salmon ladders climbed into the forested mists. Suddenly those villages, the rocky shores, the mountain backdrop seemed the most appealing places in the world. Stop, old man, I thought. Get off here. Your son is nearby, you can live anywhere, you need to get off the circuit. Find a wife, learn a language, take up calligraphy. Meditate. This life will kill you.

'Two old neurolinguists on a train to Ainu country, looking for a crippled Buddist boy,' I said.

'Some might call it a very Jewish story,' he said.

'I'll make your father an honorary Jew, wrapped in his swastika shawl.'

'You'd be a better son than I was,' he said.

Sammy wasn't in a monastery. To push an analogy, Sammy was in an attic behind a false wall, hidden and fed by strangers while agents scoured the streets looking to pick him up. He was in an old Ainu village near Sapporo, where a bearded man in robes didn't stand out so much. The monastery story was given out to save his life, because they were after him. 'Forgive me,' said Kenji. 'They were watching us.'

What about the toes, I asked. His suffering, the weight-loss, the meditation?

You might not recognize him. The body of your son is alive. The physical body endures. The primary objective was to get him out of Tokyo away from people who were trying to kill him. And to get you here, my friend. The research and lecture invitation offered a cover.

Did he ever say ... Why? I asked. How they got to him?

Cults are opportunistic feeders, said Kenji. Some of our best young people followed him. Don't blame him.

I don't, I said.

Don't blame yourself, he said.

In all the years I'd known Kenji, and in our daily contact, he never spoke to me of his wife, nor did he invite me to his house, wherever it was, for a home-cooked dinner. He had children, slightly younger than mine, of whom he spoke neither in praise nor despair. One was at home in law school, another in California getting an MBA. If he suffered on their account, if they fulfilled his dreams or haunted his nightmares, I have no idea. So far as I know, he devoted all his fatherly concerns on Sammy.

It is hard, he said, to imagine a child not wanting to have more than a father. It is hard for a father not to want to give more than he had to his child. But how can our children have more than us? How can we give them but a fraction of what we've got? I pulled the knife from my father's gut! I saw Tokyo in ashes, I buried my family, put my mother in an asylum! I promised myself to be a scientist; only science was rooted in truth, only science proceeded by hard, verifiable evidence. If I stayed with science, I would always be free. I promised my father I would learn from his blindness. I would learn from the war never to accept orders I did not personally approve – but that was easy for people like us. What of the children of fathers like you and me, who have been everywhere, seen everything, what is left that we haven't done? We can only give them scraps. Our lovely children, we showed them everything, we miniaturized the world for them, and they couldn't keep up. We should ask their forgiveness.

I clutched his hand. You've been a better father to Sammy than I have.

My country was to blame, he said.

A few minutes later he put down a book he'd been reading and asked, 'What about *in the know?* You don't say *in the feel, in the touch* ... isn't it odd?'

'In the groove, perhaps?'

'I always thought *in the nude* was a particularly regal expression,' said Kenji. 'In the Know, In the Nude. Knowledge and Nudity carry the article. It would be very interesting if English were written in Chinese characters and you had to make certain fundamental decisions about the properties of words, not just their sounds.'

'We must compare language acquisition and language retention in contrasting linguistic systems,' I said.

'So little time remains.'

There's winter-Olympics Sapporo, all Aspen glamour, and a few miles away, skidrow Sapporo, along the docks where Chinese and Koreans are smuggled in, where the tankers unload, and, if you're Kenji, you know places where the down and out, the Ainu and the *buraku* drink and find their daily labour. There is nothing strikingly different in appearance about the men knotting their nets or drinking in the harsh northern light: Japanese, Asian, lean, unkempt – in America we're so used to thinking of difference only in terms of race, or of alienation only as violence, that we're dulled to divisions that don't spit in our face or come wrapped in colour – I'm only beginning to read faces like a cop, to see in the headbands and moustaches and untrimmed beards, tattoos, the rough language, badges of identity as defiant as any gang marker on an American street. These are desperate people, my healthy respect is rooted in fear which I try not to betray, and I would not want to fall among them at night or on their terms. Sammy, I know, could be one of them, the dozing drunk, the druggie, the dull, suspicious eyes inside a darkened hut. It's been four years; I might not even recognize my own son.

Kenji speaks the language of the Ainu, or enough of it to show respect. I remember the Aborigines in Australia, the tall blond ones, the fair-skinned ones, the short, black and bearded ones – appearance doesn't matter. If you say you belong, whether you speak the language or look aboriginal or not, they take you in. The universal aboriginal brotherhood. Old men nod, and yes, they are shorter, huskier, hairier, they point us down the dockside, past dozing inebriates, the insane, the beggars. No one looks at me, or cares, I belong as much as anyone.

A long, dark warehouse of tin-topped tables squirming with squid. Faster than baskets and buckets and trolleys can dump them, teams of hunched-over, silent men and women slice and gut, steam and salt, and toss them onto conveyor belts. Many of the workers are hidden under elaborate hats, some of straw; others wear baseball caps, old hardhats. Only one is bald, with glasses, his thin, pale arms tattooed like a prisoner's. The others have all looked up, checked us out, returned to their work.

A foreman strolls over, bows to Kenji. After a few words, he departs.

'He says Sammy's his best worker. Always there, doesn't drink, doesn't use drugs, doesn't talk. No one's ever heard him talk.'

I could remember his voice, the breathless excitement after every museum visit, the endless questions. *I can hear you, Mister Beard!*

'At least he's safe here.'

'Salting squid guts. Merciful God.'

'Perhaps he'll leave with you.'

Me go pleep now.

He's still not raised his head, upon which he wears a baseball cap cocked to one side. Strike me dead on this spot, I pray, and I will praise Your justice, and Your mercy, for all eternity.

Doggystan

ONCE UPON A TIME Lander had a wife and a daughter, a dog, a teaching position and a private practice, and, so far as he thought about it, the love of his family, the respect of his neighbours and the esteem of his colleagues. If he'd defined himself in terms of descending value he might have said: husband, father, researcher, citizen.

Now, on insomniac nights between beads of sleep, he replayed his confusions, the origin of his genius, the unravelling of his life. In a cluster of years on either side of fifty, too many strangers in Lander's life had begun claiming intimacy, too many intimacies were denied connection. Some nights, impaled on that razor-wire of insomnia, he would lie awake in strange hotels, not always alone, and not remember the country he was in, the time zone or climate, or even the language. His world had become universalized to familiar hotels with CNN, universal foods and even the same sympathetic women who would hang around after a lecture on the pretence of discussing a parent's decline. He would make his way to the breakfast table, praying for skim milk and Raisin Bran but rarely finding it. Skim meant anything that would pour and raisins were embedded in a müsli-mush with the density of a collapsed star. His driver would arrive and the lectures would begin, the lab-tours, the hospital rounds, listening to Alzheimer's patients in all the world's languages, studying transcripts of the translations – if his theories were provable they had to hold up in every language – drinks and a dinner, interviews, public lectures, acolytes, women. And so he travelled.

Lander was riding a tiger, sliding from conference to conference, continent to continent, in interchangeable hotels called Ambassador or President or Intercontinental, collecting toilet kits and sleeping masks, pockets full of business cards, soaps and shampoos in small plastic bottles, as badges of his new celebrity. He used to think it was pretentious when people spoke only of airport names instead of cities, until he realized he'd become one of them, going to Logan and Laguardia, LAX or Charles de Gaulle and never into the low warehouse sprawl that radiated from them. He wanted it to end but he could not end it alone. Each flight blended into all other flights – airplane time was generic – the clock stopped when he entered the waiting room and didn't start until he had got in a taxi at the other end. Airborne existence was a wormhole connecting hundreds of calming flights, a separate existence through all his confusions. When he got back to his new Chicago highrise he'd lay out the little bottles of soapy booty and feel that they were the only tangible benefits in his new life.

Asia – the deep and mystical Asia behind the Pacific rim – was a foreign concept to him and a little frightening. He'd always resisted those Hindu and Buddhist and Muslim countries where psychoanalytic theories were considered degenerate, hysterical, or immoral parts of a neo-colonialist plot. Psychology doesn't apply to us, they'd say, we are invulnerable to your diseases of the mind: ancient wisdom combined with extended families, our faith and our natural diets make us superior to your rampant materialism, food additives and uncommitted sex. He thought of them as hypocrites, hoarders of *Playboys* worth their weight in gold in nightly rental fees back home.

This was his first trip to India. He'd avoided India in his teaching years because of encounters with skeptical students and colleagues, men (they were all men) committed to spiritual interpretations of mental disorder or some potent ayurvedic cure known only to their family's traditional quack. Freud and Jung, they were quick to remind him, had both insulted Asia, deeming it psychologically savage or infantile. The only way of remedying his mentor's ancient wrong was for him – Freud's direct intellectual descendant, according to popular belief – to do them the courtesy of proving they were as sick, and for the same reasons, as everyone else. And so at last and with nothing to fear he had agreed on this brief lecture and demonstration tour of India squeezed between residencies in Japan and Israel.

Mangy dogs lay like piles of oily rags, fused as tight and still as roadkill to the pavement. Dr Dalal slalomed between them to his gate. Perhaps, Lander thought, since the street dogs of India were no longer bred for human vanity this was the way all dogs would choose to look: grungy patches of dun and white somewhere between jackal and retriever. Hell, thought Lander, it's the way I would choose to look.

Lander, a lifelong dog-man, shopper at dog pounds, adopter of lost causes, defender of mongrels, found these dogs threatening and unappealing – even the bandy-legged pups still sucking on a bitch's teat just inches from his feet as he got out of Dalal's car. She growled. As in all things he'd observed in his first few days in India, fertility was raw and naked, neither maternity nor infancy having a thing to do with benevolence or play or cuteness, no respite from mange and filth.

Two weeks in India, however – to give the dogs credit – and he'd not seen a street dog, whatever its deprivation, attack a child, a kid-goat, calf or piglet, despite their mutual unsupervised foraging through the same stacks of gutter refuse. He could not say the same about Westchester purebreds, where Judy had raised showdogs before the breakup. Street dogs belonged to no one yet they were partially looked after and partially loyal, beneficiaries of indifferent scraps of shade, water and tolerance, attached loosely to houses or shops. They responded not with gratitude but aggressive territoriality, the poor man's watchdog. This was Gujarat, a meatless state, and the dogs had adjusted to a vegetarian diet.

'Protective, not aggressive,' said Dr Dalal, president of the All-India Psychological Association, as he stepped over a dog and slid open the metallic latch to his front gate. Dalal was fifty, an august name in Indian research though not exactly on Lander's wavelength. Dalal had spent too many years in the Freudian trenches proselytizing for broad classical psychiatry. He had become too committed to the classic outlines to tolerate much revision. His three-piece-silk-suit orthodoxy, his trimmed moustache and dyed black hair had made Lander yearn for stubble-chinned, henna-dyed, wild-eyed ayurvedic practitioners in stained dhotis crying out as they had at his first lecture in Calcutta: Forget genes. Forget APO-E4. Study the true cure, *Ashwagandha*. Study *Bramhi, Shankhapushpi, Vacha*.

On the distant front porch behind rose bushes, across a patchy, browning lawn, he noticed a tall slim woman in a white sari holding the leashes of two large howling white dogs. She was too far away for Lander to note her appearance, only that he didn't have to. She was clad, or wrapped, in a white sari that for all its modesty might have been unblemished Grecian nudity. She seemed part of a master's miniature painting rendered in delicate strokes by a single camel's hair. Even at a distance he could count the stones of her necklace, the gold carving on her bangle. He knew she would be as beautiful as her husband was ordinary. Her voice and manner and accent would charm as much as his had irritated. He knew it because of her profile as she turned to go back inside before dropping the dogs' chains. He was staring. It was a mythic moment.

'Dr Lander, bringing her into my life, at my age, you understand, has undermined everything I believed. That's why I became attracted to your work, sir. It somehow ennobled what I had done, even while I was feeling the deepest shame. You cannot know how I ... well, the suffering I have caused. I was a married man with children. I had many of the things I had worked for. Bringing her into my life was like bringing in the future, or maybe the past, discovering the superhuman ... well, I cannot explain it.'

In an instant Lander was ripped from a timeless world of the woman on the porch, the confessor at his side, to an explosion of dust as the two dogs leaped the rose bushes and propelled themselves, jaws foaming, tongues flapping, eyes pinpointed with hate, to a snapping, snarling halt inches in front of Lander's shoes.

Dr Dalal reached out his hand perhaps to be licked, or snatched away.

'Crude, but lovable,' he said.

Old scabs and fresh scratches laced his forearm more like an indulgent cat-owner's than a dog-fancier's. 'We took them from the street when their eyes were still closed. You saw their sister just outside the gate. Such dogs are blessed with sweet natures, you'll find, despite appearances. My wife ways we should not call them dogs at all.'

What then? Lander wondered. Jackals, pariahs?

Dalal laughed, reading his confusion. 'Canines, Dr Lander.

Dogs are domesticated canines. Canines are immigrants into the country of dogs.'

Whatever they were, they were large and strong, front legs and shoulders bunched with muscle, faces broad and intelligent with long, overdeveloped muzzles and powerful jaws rehearsing a full repertoire of Alsatian, Labrador, and Dobermann ancestry – they could pull sleds, or carts, or tear burglars into small pieces – while their sloping, apologetic hindquarters with fluffy tails curled along their backs betrayed generations of back-alley encounters with wild and degenerate breeds. The whole mixture struck Lander as heroic and unfortunate, the abject, sexually excited tail-wagging, the foamy-jawed growling, the ferocious timidity of a confused enthusiasm.

'Loyal, but untrainable,' said Dr Dalal.

After the tea and fresh fruit juices served at the landscaped border of a pond and waterfall, after the tour of the house, the work of a foreign-trained local architect, with its panelled walls of modern Indian paintings, its CD-trees of American rock, Indian ragas and Western classics, at the dinner table, Lata Dalal asked Lander, 'What do you know about zebra mollusks?' They were nearly finished with dinner, an elaborate and elegant vegetarian spread attended by the dogs whom both Dalals fed rice balls, chapattis, and bits of peas and potato samosa. Lander had finally asked her, now that he could face her beauty directly and not hide his enchantment, what exactly she was researching.

'Ah, biology,' he said.

'I'm a sociologist,' she said, 'so I am very interested in zebra mollusks. They've nearly turned San Francisco Bay into the Dead Sea.'

'Lata did her doctorate at Berkeley,' explained Dr Dalal.

'Forgive my confusion –' said Lander, '– but mollusks and sociology?'

'Prakash rescued me from marriage,' she said.

'No, my dear. I rescued you from divorce.'

'From the endless round of fucking and being fucked. Prakash is my third. The usual story – ambitious girl from good family is stuck with an arranged marriage, goes through with it, tries suicide, gets divorced, goes to America, falls in love with the first American she sleeps with, marries him. All the usual boring details, finds out he's the usual –'

'– cheating mollusk?' asked Lander.

'– mollusks are actually rather noble in a good-of-the-race, self-sacrificing way – no, it was more the armed robbery and drug-dealing. There is such a thing as too much America. So, she divorces and rebounds and rebounds, a boring story, no? Loving and being loved is so much better, isn't it, Dr Lander?' Her voice was hoarse and throaty, her accent a complicated confection, rather like a cuisine that offered no familiar openings. Her hand had risen to his arm, the flesh cool, silky, but the wrists scabbed like her husband's. A jagged white scar was barely covered by a watch and gold bangles.

'You've had some rough times, haven't you?'

She glanced to her wrist, and smiled. 'From my first night in jail.'

'Dalal means middleman,' said the doctor. 'We are all traders by caste, not professionals. My father and brother think I should be running an import business in Flushing or Southall.'

'Lander just means farmer, or a person from a particular place.'

'On the street, Dalal means pimp,' said Lata. 'You can't escape your calling.'

'Lata is very direct, you'll notice.'

'What about those zebra mollusks?' he asked.

'I am writing on the transformation of Indian society by the presence of millions of what we call NRIs – non-resident Indians – either returning to India from years abroad, remitting money, or visiting. Every smuggled computer is a zebra mollusk. Every child who disobeys his parents is a mollusk. Every daughter who marries for love. Every VCR, every western adult film is a mollusk, every labour-saving device, every vacuum cleaner, every coffee-maker, is a servant-killing mollusk. The servants respond, poor things, and become treacherous thieves and vandals, or worse. In Berkeley I studied the Indian community in America. Isn't it interesting that men without two rupees to rub together in India become millionaires in Texas? Do you know there are villages not ten miles from here where ninety percent of the able-bodied population is in England, Canada or the United States? It's people from here who own your motels and 7-11s. I don't think you'll meet a person in India who doesn't have intimate family living abroad, or who hasn't studied there or isn't planning to send his children to Harvard and Stanford – zebra mollusks are very adaptable. They were sucked into the ballast tanks of the big oil tankers in Japan and their larvae got expelled at the Oakland docks. They have no natural enemies.'

The only question would be, Lander thought, how to spend two nights in the Dalal house without obsessing over Lata Dalal, wherever she might be at any moment, where she slept, what she thought of him.

'We are intermediate life-forms, Dr Lander,' she said. 'What would you call this house with all its comforts and conveniences – India? And yet where else do we belong? What else do you call us?'

'Like these creatures,' said Dr Dalal. 'Are they dogs? They are enacting in just one or two years the whole history of their species' domestication.'

'They are immigrants to Doggystan,' said Lata Dalal. 'A brand new country. Just like all of us.'

The male had begun climbing, cat-like, up Lata's ladderback chair, laying his head on the top rung where he licked her neck and softly moaned while humping the scroll-work at the back of the seat, the sloping hindquarters marvellously fluid in their piston-like pumping, the bright pink glistening member erupting with each thrust to brush against the pleats of her sari. It seemed like a frieze out of Khajuraho. The bitch at Dr Dalal's feet had maneuvered herself to take full advantage of his naked toes.

'Shoo-shoo,' she cooed, kissing his muzzle. 'Don't make a nuisance.'

'Knock knock,' said Lander.

'I beg your pardon?' asked Dr Dalal.

'Ah ... who's there?' said Lata.

'Ayurvedic,' said Lander.

'Ayurvedic who?' she asked.

'Ayurvedic for the doctah?' he giggled.

They had drained the bottles of imported wine and local brandy. The dogs had retired to the porch, Lata and Dr Dalal shared the couch, Lander sat in a leather chair. American music had given way to distant ragas. Indian languages, closer to the origin of western speech than any others, were discussed: perhaps Sanskritic roots, thought Dr Dalal – pre-industrial, pre-literate, with compound nouns and heavily inflected verbs – supported Lander's theories. In his current state, tipsy and infatuated and living inside an erotic sculpture, all theories made equal sense. If civilization now permitted us to live longer than our bodies' programmes, if we accepted the toll in cancer and heart disease, diabetes and bad eyesight, weight and arthritis as inevitable, why shouldn't our brains outlive their language programme? If there is less Alzheimer's in India – and there is, Dr Lander – it is not because of food and ancient wisdom; perhaps it is only the languages we speak and lack of overload. We don't have to process as much. Perhaps, who knows, we will find that one picture is worth a thousand words and that thirty years of television exhausts the brain, destroys its linguistic capacity. Crashes its RAM, so to speak. Dalal was coming alive, Lata was drowsing, the dogs were scratching the door, and Lander was as close to non-existence as he had ever felt.

The language of Alzheimer's patients appears to share common traits, he heard himself agreeing. The so-called Lander grammar. Yes, cried Dalal, clapping his hands and startling his wife: There are tribal languages in India, older than Sanskrit, that anticipate all the rules of Alzheimer's speech. Pronouns of attribute not of persona, verbs of recent position not movement. You sit on a stool in front of a man and he calls you Broad-Shouldered Friend with One Eye. He says, Broad-Shouldered Man with One Eye brings fish to Fat Woman's table. But those people aren't there and there is no fish, no woman and no table. You are fully sighted and slope-shouldered, see, Dr Lander? Languages whose present can only be expressed as the past, self that has no grammatical marker at all.

Ontogeny recapitulates philology, thought Lander, filing it away.

His brain was softening, turning to mush, he could sleep for a week.

Lata Dalal stood, and held her arms out to him. He rose, took her by the tips of her fingers. 'My room is just across from yours,' she said. 'I am a bit unsteady. Please take me.'

'I'll be along directly, Lata,' called her husband.

Outside his door she delivered a kiss and a cool hand on the back of his neck. He could imagine their bodies flowing together, like rubble from collapsed walls. 'Please feel free to call if there's anything you need.'

'Dr Dalal?'

'I sleep alone.'

'Then perhaps – I know this is bold – you will feel free to call on me.'

At first she smiled, considering her options. 'And which of us is the mollusk, Dr Lander? And who is the bay?'

He felt a dog slither past him in the hall.

For his first thirty-five years, his innocent and luminous years, he had missed a great deal by not seeing everything as sexual, every woman as a potential partner. In his next twenty, he had thought of little else. It had ruined his good name, his dignity, his pride. It had brought no peace. These feelings at his age were unseemly. Lata turned, raised a hand in half a wave, her bangles jangling, and disappeared inside the darkened room.

Lander began undressing. Early in his travels a Russian woman had told him, we have killed what it means to have humanity. Jews had it and we killed them. Christians had it and we killed them. Old-style Russian peasants had it and we killed them, too. Now all we have are half-men and half-women who never knew what it was to be human.

We used to know, Lander had said. We're losing it, too.

Poor you, she'd said.

I want to be whole.

In the darkest night of his life in a room so still and black that he couldn't tell if his eyes were closed or open he awoke to the rustle of bedclothes, the white body assuming her place on the adjacent pillow, folding her legs, crossing her arms, eyes imploring. The proof of all his theories was upon him. It was one of those nights when he could believe there was no madness, no disease in the world, only new languages to discover. And so that way they spent the night, his stiffened cock up the bitch's cunt, her jaw clamped firmly on his wrist.

Dark Matter

A NORMAL LIFE OF EIGHTY YEARS can be expressed as a parabola, like the equations you graphed on little blue squares in ninth-grade algebra when you had no idea that the points you plotted and the lines connecting them, peaking at forty and falling away, were the picture of your life.

Lander's current coördinates placed him at midpoint on the downslope. As a man of sixty with strong genes for the heart, dubious ones for long-term consciousness, he could bet on ten more years of research and adventure followed by a decade of confusion and decline. Playing the back nine, as it were, midway through the thirteenth hole, bunkers and sandtraps, doglegs right and left, clubhouse in view, but when he got there this time, there'd be no nineteenth hole, no gin and tonic on the deck.

'Do you like pears, Dr Lander?' his escort, David Fisher, asked. Fisher, a publicist from the American embassy, had been assigned to Lander for the conference. Fisher cultivated the local look: orchestra conductor on a summer break, white shirt hanging out, sandals, sleeves rolled up, bushy grey hair in need of grooming. They were waiting in the crowded, smoky lobby of a fancy hotel in the middle of Tel Aviv for the arrival of a childhood friend of Lander's whom he could not have recognized or avoided. Fisher was there to see that Lander didn't get lost, bored or bothered. Fisher flashed a chrome-plated switchblade and carved a dainty sliver of glistening pear which he balanced on the blade.

'I grew it myself,' he said.

Halfway between forty and death, Lander mused, matches a point halfway between birth and apogee. Lander at sixty, in Israel for a conference on 'The Human Language, Economics to Theology,' was staring directly through a time-tunnel at his twenty-year-old self, the boy he'd been when he'd visited the Promised Land for the first time.

Yoo-hoo, kid!

'We lease twenty hectares from a kibbutz up on the Golan,'

Fisher continued. 'I'm taking early retirement and staying here.' He plopped a knit yarmulke over his convenient bald spot, then pocketed it just as quickly, with a wink. 'I tell them I've got a place in Beth Ezra and they hear it as Bethesda. It's better that way.'

'*Aliyah* at our age? You're a brave man.'

'Pears belong in Eretz, don't you think?'

This time, Lander took the proffered pear. Sweet, firm, a Chosen Fruit. Fisher's own patented Sabra-sounding cross-breed, green-flecked, golden-skinned with overtones of red.

'I really despise oranges, those greedy little sun-suckers. Remember Jaffas?'

'I do indeed,' said Lander.

'Pears get firm in the wind and sweet in the cold. Pears need the Golan, Dr Lander.'

'A regular foreign policy fruit.'

'Precisely. When you finish eating an orange what have you got? Skin, seeds, pulp and all that disgusting white matter – am I right, or am I right? What's left after you eat a pear, Dr Lander?'

'Evidently very little, Mr Fisher.'

He suddenly remembered his mother bathing him in the old Brooklyn kitchen. The radio was on, she singing. Crosby, Andrews Sisters, or was that too early? Before the war. She rolled back the wrinkled skin at the tip of his tiny penis: *Wash here, sweetie, learn to do it yourself. See the white matter that sticks in there. You don't want to get an infection.* Belly-button, too. White matter. Earwells. Eyegunk. Your comb, curls of old toilet paper up your butt.

'My point exactly. Sweet and firm, packs well, ships anywhere. I even eat the seeds.' He made an eloquent throat-clearing noise that Lander had not heard in forty years. 'Oranges and bananas, they were Russian dream fruits. *Venn ve're free, den ve plant orange trees!* Oranges are diaspora. They should have stayed in Florida.'

'So all the fruits are political?'

'Why shouldn't they be?' Fisher answered.

And is every question answered with a question? He didn't ask.

Little did you think, Jerry, or Gershy as they called you in that heroic *Exodus* summer of '56, that every twenty-year-old is spied on by his inner old man. Little did I think, looking at those rugged old kibbutzniks, that every sixty-year-old is still the kid inside. It's the opposite of nostalgia. As though memory were a function of youth, not old age. What you plant is what you remember. It was Lander's basic thesis: Nothing is lost, no gesture in the universe goes unretained.

'More pear? I brought plenty.'

When he was twenty and Israel eight, Lander spent a summer packing oranges in an English-speaking kibbutz near the Lebanon border with mostly New York and Montréal kids whose grandparents wintered in the same Florida ghettos – affirming identity, defending the land, falling in love and nearly staying. But Davia Appelbaum, his first great love, who could roll cigarettes with one hand while strumming chords with the other and still lead folk-songs in African click-languages, reckless lovemaker on any lumpy horizontal surface and against quite a few vertical ones, behind, or on top of packing boxes where the fragrance of just-picked Jaffas and the memory of stolen passion would kickstart his mornings for the next forty years – that Davia Appelbaum had giant ambitions.

She, *dear boy*, was only passing through, from Jo'burg to London. Israel's sinewy farmers and citizen-soldiers reminded her of back-country Boers, pistol on hip, trussed with bandoleers; they would never create an urban culture. She'd left South Africa at sixteen with no intention of waiting for majority rule and the inevitable slaughter of whites and Indians. Constant preparedness was the enemy of all creation.

Lander returned to his junior year at Chicago. They wrote for a few months. He cherished her letters, the only tangible sign, to that time, that he'd had a life. He found himself going to small theatres and jazz clubs and was freshly drawn to a folk-scene he'd always ignored. She was singing, acting, discarding identities and lovers. Not to be outdone, he declared a psychology major. That appeared to be the great legacy of Israel in his life; a taste for performance, a premature embrace of the sixties, an appreciation for Joan Baez, a weakened strain of the Appelbaum virus.

And now he couldn't remember enough Hebrew even to sound out the street signs. You'd think, after all these centuries of careful inbreeding, a mutant gene for reading Hebrew would arise. Of course, it's a different Hebrew, Fisher had reminded him, Torah piety crossed with army profanity. He'd even come to Israel without a hat.

All Lander could remember from his attempts at mastering the sacred language was the panic of memorizing passages in an unheated annex to the temple library where he and three other boys, Marty Fogelman, whose father paid for the *melamed,* Arnie Zucker, and a strange boy named Anatol, sat after school with a glyptodon from Lublin, a distant relative of the Fogelmans. Even in that cold room he wore short-sleeved white shirts, better to expose the tattoos with the European barred sevens on the underside of his frail white arms. *See what happens?* those numbers said.

He'd been Gershy in temple, and it was as Gersh that he'd received a note on impressive stationery from (now) Ari Zucker. *Dear Gersh: Saw the write-up in the paper, fancy company! Nobel Prizes and all, a guy I went to school with, I'm impressed, really. I came to Eretz in '72. Married Leah here, three kids, all smart like their mother. You remember what an ox I was. Let me show you the family, the stores. Life's been good. Maybe I didn't make it as big in Brooklyn as I said I would, but try to buy an appliance in Tel Aviv without me.*

Back in Brooklyn, Arnie Zucker's only ambition had been to capitalize on his A to Z initials. He'd been a throwback to the peddler-era, no law school, no medicine, no teaching in his family or his future. A to Z Hardware, Radio Repair, Shirts and Suits.

Lander was not a Nobel laureate, could never be, given the nature of his work. He was often introduced as a Nobel Prize winner, a mistake nearly impossible to rectify once it was made. He wanted to print it on his card: *Gerald Lander, Clinical Psychologist. No Prizes Worth Mentioning.* The other conference participants, natural scientists, economists, writers, were nearly all Nobel winners. Witty, modest, cultured people. He wondered if they were as lost as he.

According to the conference brochure, disciplines may start out modestly, corrections and footnotes to prevailing opinion, but as they mature they begin to offer totalizing explanations of their own. The interaction and conditioning of social groups, the inherent patterning of myth, the exchange value of productive labour, sociobiology; call it language-making, brain-chemistry or the subconscious, they all point feebly at times, insistently at others, toward a god, or away from it. Since moving between disciplines opens an intellectual to charges of dilettantism, it was thought that the conference itself could serve as the forum. Let the audience make the connections.

So why not Israel, home of dispute, where everyone's an expert, where intellectuals strike public poses, where ideas have immediacy, in a city where gods and language came together and split apart? It was time for him to find out. An assimilated, diasporic, Jew – on which word does the emphasis fall? Israel was either the purest and most concentrated form of his experience, or its total denial.

A fawn-coloured Cadillac pulled into the portico.

'Your ride,' said Fisher, pocketing the switchblade and dropping a slim pear core inside a napkin into the ashtray. 'Shall we say after the conference next Sunday at Beth Ezra? I'll pick you up in Jerusalem. My wife's anxious to meet you, too.'

'That would be fine.'

'We'll send you all the tapes of the conference. Anything you need, the embassy will provide.'

'Thank you, Mr Fisher.'

'Dovid,' he said.

The bigger the car the smaller the driver had been Lander's observation on trips to Florida, and Ari Zucker was no exception. Lander immediately remembered him, unchanged from half a century: a wiry little guy with thick arms, shirt out, knit yarmulke, shooing the valet-parker away, ignoring the doorman's salute. Lander rose to meet him, this boy from Brooklyn who'd meant absolutely nothing to him fifty years ago but who'd suddenly thrust himself back in his life. The second time as tragedy, was that the formula, third time as farce? Everything in his life was gently folding over, everything a replay.

'Gershy!'

Arnie had a still-young face, less weathered than many he'd seen. He'd kept his hair, unlike Lander, and all but the temples was suspiciously black. His forearms were a real kibbutznik's, stretching the links of a gold watchband. Lander was embraced, pawed, thumped, lifted, he felt loved and tribal, desert and Mediterranean all at once, plucked from the polite company of the conference and into the companionship of something all-forgiving, all-demanding, Mafia-like, direct and earthy.

Ignoring the horns and shouts of drivers he'd blocked, Zucker took him to the street outside the hotel, pointing out the storefront just across, its frontage loud with sheets of fluorescent tubing, turning half the block studio-bright on a Sunday afternoon.

'All my stores get the same treatment, Gershy. It's a Japanese technique. Brighter than a thousand suns. Hop in, I'll tell you a story.'

Zucker was determined to show him the city, and to take him past as many Zuckerlands as he could. After a while, Lander could sense their approach, something hot and glowing in the distance. 'Mossad came to me two years ago. Very serious guys, Mossad. Said the American spy satellite told them we were conducting some kind of laser-testing. All this heat, all this light in Tel Aviv and Jerusalem. So they lay out a city-grid, plot the so-called sites and guess what: Twenty-two Zuckerlands! I'm in space, who needs a web-site?' Then his expression soured. 'If I could write "Fuck you, Hafez el-Clinton" in the biggest lights in the world, I would.'

He wheeled down a narrow, market-lined street, glaring at the vision of Arab stalls, piles of vegetables, breads and clothing spilling out into the street. 'They won't be happy till they turn us into another Third World country,' he muttered, honking away the Arabs, cursing their slowness, their sheer numbers. 'They'd slit your throat for a shekel. You can smell them!' Lander winced, trapped in his golden, air-conditioned cage of a Cadillac which had never seemed so uselessly large, wishing he could lose himself in the swirl of street life.

'Did you read about the bomb on the bus? My accountant lost his wife in it. Twenty-five years old, just married, or does Jewish blood make the papers in America?'

'I read, I saw,' said Lander.

'So, it sells.'

Arnie Zucker's American life had been a failure so vast he'd even enlisted in the Vietnam War, waiving deferments, pulling strings, hoping to die. So what happened? They made him a procurement officer. He prospered, saw opportunities, tapped the possibilities. 'I was thirty-two years old, you'd probably won your Nobel Prize by then, and what was I doing? Well, actually, ashamed to say but I'm making out pretty good. Had my own apartment in Saigon, selling air-conditioners right off the ship. Then I woke up one morning and it hit me: I'm fighting *their* war. Simple as that.'

'Whose war?'

'Exactly. Westmoreland, some redneck from Carolina. McNamara? Johnson? Nixon? Those were teachers' names for God's sake! They could have been Japanese.' He leaned across the wide front seat. 'I tell you this, Gersh, it's America that's killing us. They'll sacrifice us for oil. What America's doing to us makes Hitler a drop in the bucket.'

'Don't get crazy on me, Arnie.'

'Ari.'

When he came out he packed his bags for Israel, arrived in time for the '72 War, rose to captain and met the money men from Buenos Aires who initially set him up. He saw himself as a nation-builder, wiring the desert, if only for cable TV.

'Here, at least wear this,' he said, pressing a knit yarmulke into Lander's hands. 'Bet you haven't worn one in ... what, twenty years?'

'You call me Hitler one minute then you give me this?'

'When, Holy Days? Bar-mitzvahs? Shiva?'

'Don't turn Forty-seventh Street on me, Ari.'

'What, now you feel ashamed? Typical diaspora reaction. Wear it, okay?'

'I'm bald, it slides – you got the same model in Velcro?'

Could one live in Israel with a sliding yarmulke, with ambivalence? The most precious thing in the world to Lander was his belonging to a place that subtly excluded him – or was it his right to reject a place that subtly included him? Israel was a club he wished would reject him.

Ari kept up a steady commentary. Lander was accustomed to being the object of questions; Ari Zucker was as unimpressed by intellectual accomplishment as he'd ever been. No questions about his work, about his life, family, loves, travels. Only one trip counted, and that was the passage to Israel.

'What, our facilities are bad? Students aren't smart?'

'No complaints, Arnie.'

'Ari – if you don't mind. So, come. You're never too old. Get an apartment somewhere. What, didn't your parents teach you a Jew should always keep a bag packed?

These fierce old parents that everyone quotes, where do they come from? Lander suspected that most people, himself included, were in the parent-manufacturing business. He remembered Arnie Zucker's parents and his own as the ultimate get-along types, New Dealers, benignly liberal in the abstract, a little jumpy after the first robberies, the graffiti, the name-calling. But giving up America, packing a bag, making *aliyah?* That was for the relatives left behind, the second and third choice after America and maybe Canada. Down there with South Africa and Argentina. Australia wasn't bad for Jews who surfed.

'Christ, Arnie, Ari, I'd sit around like those *alte kockers* in Brighton Beach, sipping *glayzl chai* and moaning about Odessa.'

'What, you're more the beer and schnapps type? *Hey, Germans love me, this Hitler guy's a joke.*'

'Get something straight, Ari. History isn't a recording.'

'What, for Jews it's one big loop, Gershy, you get that straight. For you, what, history's a laugh track? America loves you, gives you all these prizes? Anyway, why should you worry, they'll never come for you, will they? You're too valuable.'

'I resent your tone.'

'What, my tone? We're an abrasive people. We don't back down, get that straight. Russia backed down. Israel never. I'll do anything it takes to get through to you. Or do you want to go quietly?'

They cruised in silence through suburban streets that could have been not quite California, maybe Florida if Florida had slopes. They corkscrewed up the hills, the houses clinging like California chalets for purchase on a bit of grass and flowers, a stone wall, sudden views of the Mediterranean. Every stone was biblical, every old tree had borne witness, withstood the Ottomans, the Mandate, and welcomed the ancient owners back. It was in the blood, even

Lander could feel it, be caught up in it, the mystical attachment, the martyrdoms, the ritualized landscape.

Nothing disruptive in these elevations, no Arabs, less noise, more strollers and baby carriages, more children out, more men in hats. Lander had avoided Israel for forty years for the same reason he avoided moral knuckle-rappers and religious authority. The right wing, wherever he encountered it, made his skin crawl. But if he were a debater, he'd rather argue the side of human depravity, the inevitability of catastrophe, the genetic hostility of disparate ethnicities, than any accommodationist position.

'By the way, did you see the Million Man March? A million black men hate your sorry ass.'

'I was travelling.'

'Very nice. So, how long you think you've got before they come for you?'

'They?'

'How many blacks in America now, how many Spanish, how many of those *meshugge* Christians? Fifteen, twenty, twenty-five per cent – you got over half of your countrymen *that want you dead*. You ran the slave ships, you were Christopher Columbus, you nailed up their Messiah. That Million Man March scared the shit out of me, and I've been in three wars.'

'Lighten up, Ari.'

'I've made my money, I looked after the family, I brought my parents over and buried them here. I've fought for two countries. Now, only the survival of my people matters to me. I can meet any price. Even if *you* don't care, I do.'

Arnie's home was a low, California-style ranch occupying the top of a steep hill. No neon, no flags, nothing showy or unusual. An artful tangle of semi-desert plants, bright flowers, low trees, rocks and sand gave the illusion of more space than it actually occupied.

A stooped old woman in a babushka and buttoned sweater kept up a sullen sweeping of the stepping stones. A man, short and thick, her husband perhaps, clipped roses along a trellis. Their deeply lined faces suggested peasantry, the Balkans, those faces of the ethnically cleansed.

'Shalom, Figs.'

‘’lom,’ he muttered.

Wraparound windows commanded a three-sided view of the ocean and the blocks of houses and switchback roads rising from the city to the south, and to the north the long sweep of the ocean studded with developments as far as vision permitted. No English magazines on the coffee table, no English books in the bookcases. Ari poured out two small glasses of a dark fluid; Israeli cognac perhaps.

‘We owe those people out there, Gershy,’ said Zucker. ‘Bosnians. They’re suffering for us.’

‘Agreed.’

‘I’m glad you do. The Jews of Europe.’

‘Bosnian Jews?’

‘*Real* Jews, Gershy, the only real Jews left in Europe. What’s a real Jew, tell me that?’

‘I don’t need this, Arnie. You’re not my rabbi.’ The cognac was dry, surprisingly good.

‘What, need? We’re just two old friends debating a serious question. Rationally, God forbid we should be emotional. What is a real Jew and how do you know him? It’s simple. A real Jew is known by his enemies.’

These Old Testament types, always right, never in doubt, was it something in the water? He saw where it was going, even as Ari bulled ahead.

‘So, who hates that poor old couple out there the most? Germans, naturally, since they back the Croats, Americans and the *New* OPEC *Times* and Khomeini News Network since they all back the Muslims. There’s the Afghans and the Turks and the Iranians and Arafat’s boys and don’t forget Muhammed Clintonov, who bombs them. Who’s defending Europe against the Iranians? Who, Gershy, who?’

My enemy’s enemy.

‘Serbs,’ he sighed.

‘Serbs. I’d bring the whole Bosnian Serb army over here if I could. A little ethnic cleansing is what we need. Instead, you’re cleansing us – America! Moving Jews off our land! I never thought I’d see the day, America and Syria against Israel. Old Figs – that’s all he eats now, figs stewed in condensed milk – old Figs was a company commander. Lost his sons, lost his house, his daughter was raped by Muslims in front of her mother. The old lady hasn't said a word in two years. Bet you don't read that in the OPEC *Times* – Arab oil money buys them off.'

And just as his neck cords were popping, his voice rising, Leah Haddad, fresh from her shower, entered the room. Ari sat, smiled, and seemed to shrink. She was petite and dark-eyed, Tunisian. The rest of the Haddads had moved to Paris and Montréal; she'd been the only one to move east to the maternal bosom. She took him on a tour of the house, her study, their paintings and manuscripts. She was a theatre and gallery patron, a collector and preserver. Nothing in Israel lacked a story, a history, its own private suffering. In her presence, Ari was a man of few and mild opinions, respectful of Lander's books, which Leah had been reading in their French editions.

'Such an honour having you here, even so briefly,' Ari declared, as Figs served platters of cakes and tea, the hectoring gone. In its place, the familiar tone of respect that Lander had come to expect, and distrust, in the world.

'When Ari said he knew you, I almost doubted him. *Almost*,' she flirted, 'didn't I?'

'It's strange, you gotta admit,' said Ari. 'A *zhlub* like me knowing a *kopf* like him – it really don't figure.'

'That was Brooklyn in those days,' said Lander.

'Remember Anatol Kirshbaum?' Ari suddenly interjected, 'the guy who went to Hollywood?'

'Yeah, right, I've been trying to remember that name. What ever happened?'

'Don't you know?' Leah jumped in. 'Andy Kirkwood?'

'Andy Kirkwood, Jesus,' and now for the first time in the day Lander could laugh. What a tribe, what a community. Andy Kirkwood was the runty little guy who'd made neurosis sexy.

'He came over to open our new civic theatre,' said Leah. 'Ari's contact.'

'And a new Zuckerland. Cut the ribbon on that store I first showed you. Stayed in your hotel, came up here, sat right there.

He's a serious guy in real life. Said he thinks of settling here all the time.'

'With his problems, I might too.'

'He misses the old language. Misses the sun. He buried his parents here, their request.'

So what can you say? If Marty Fogelman, king of the bypass, had lived – lung cancer took him out twenty years ago, a brilliant doctor who should have known better – that little Hebrew class had paid some heavy debts, given some pleasure, kept the faith in different ways.

'It's been good,' said Lander.

'What? This afternoon, this life, what?'

At the conference that began in Jerusalem the next day, Lander found himself grouped with the linguists and brain-mappers, but more attracted to the writers and economists. Five years after his work on the recovery of meaning in severe dementia, he was still the Alzheimer's man, though his new concerns were elsewhere.

What is meant by memory? Memory had always been considered involuntary, a kind of passive default position. You can't *not* have memory, even, if you accept Lander's hypothesis, in all but the final stage of Alzheimer's. But what if memory were a construction, or at least constructable, and not just a residue of past experience? Certain cultures still had it, certain languages still embodied it. Songlines, sweat-lodges, dream-quests. Bar-mitzvahs, he was tempted to say, without the shmaltzy songs and tables of pastrami. What if one were to have vivid memories of future events? So vivid even the young could be guided by them? His speculations were drawing him dangerously close to mysticism, a fact he was not ready to share with his colleagues and audience.

In the spirit of the conference, he too was edging towards a unified vision. If he had stated it boldly it would have caused headlines: Man at one time had clairvoyance. There are languages, cultures, that draw no distinctions between future, past and present. Of course we call them primitive. We have evolved, retaining at best a vestige of ancient memory called merely anticipation. We wait for the pleasure of making memories of the future.

Anticipation and memory. Is what we anticipate also what we remember? Are they matching points on the same parabola? His mother had died, essentially, of starvation, unable to remember the taste or texture of food, unable to anticipate its arrival. Just a hot or a cold object thrust into her mouth; no wonder she let it dribble away. If nothing else, Lander's talk elevated anticipation to new heights of seriousness. He heard it referred to the next day as *anticipationality*. It was even called *anticipation theory*, which aroused the interest of certain economists.

There was, in the world of macroeconomics, a ratio known as Kaminsky's constant, which had earned Joel Kaminsky a Nobel in the first years that they had been awarded to economists. In the profession, Kaminsky was called the Prince of Darkness for his interest in the utility of waste, corruption, and other unsavoury elements of economic activity. *In Praise of Corruption* was a kind of dark shadow of Galbraith's *Affluent Society*, or even, some said, a direct descendant of Machiavelli. Kaminsky by now was well over eighty, luxuriantly eyebrowed, stooped and lean, travelling with a much younger Asian woman called 'Kaminsky's second constant'. It was Kaminsky who sought out Lander, sending a message to meet him for coffee.

He liked to call himself a simple gardener, though he still consulted for governments wishing to ascertain the magnitude of their hidden economies. When he and Lander compared travel notes, it became apparent that Lander was the stay-at-home. The world he travelled was comparatively safe and well-lit, the comforts of home nearly replicated. Kaminsky's world, by choice, took him to villages, through squalid back alleys, to the loading docks and train stations of the Third World. He was the Mahatma Gandhi of self-imposed discomfort.

Kaminsky's lecture had been 'Towards a Theory of Economic Dark Matter'. In astronomy, we subtract the visible and known weight of the universe from what – according to all our theories of light and gravity and motion – our calculations tell us must still be out there, unseen. You start with a huge number, you subtract a huge number, and you come up with a huge number for what must be the invisible weight of the universe. The so-called dark matter, the stuff that's as heavy as everything we can see, only we have to take even its existence on a kind of theoretical faith.

Well, the economy is a little like celestial mechanics. It yields some astonishing numbers. There appear to be mysterious forces that bind an economy together ('I called them *feygelehs* once, and it popped up in very sober Japanese journal, so I'm careful about giving names to anything,' he said), and there are forces that fling it apart. As in all things great and small, no? Marriages, families, even the human mind, if I understand your work, Dr Lander. The older I get, the more I see the universe working its same Manichean magic everywhere. Light and Dark. Everywhere, there's dark matter. Without it, we'd just sail into infinity. Is an economy capable of infinite expansion like the universe? Or does it reach a point when all coherence is lost, when market laws are no longer operable? Will we crunch up into a little ball?

Is that a workable model for the mind, for memory, as well, Dr Lander? I leave it to you.

Kaminsky discounted the difficulty of his theory. 'Like calculating the existence of Pluto by studying the orbit of Neptune. It's all trigonometry,' said the Prince of Darkness. 'That's where it started, Brooklyn Tech, trying to work out sines and cosines for something more interesting than ladders against the sides of buildings. I didn't count on the military interest, but that's another story.

'I anticipate your next question, Dr Lander. The cleanest real country in the world is Iceland, after dear old Singapore, of course, which isn't real at all. Angela's Singaporean,' he said, causing his ex-student to blush. 'Singapore gives us the baseline. We know everything's accounted for, nothing's wasted or diverted. There are no jay-walkers, economically speaking. But no dark matter is a perfectly wretched way to live, in my opinion. We need our darkness, don't we? Shadows make us human. Norway's good, all the usual Scandinavian virtues. New Zealand, too. Is a pattern emerging? I hope so. The U.S., Mexico and China have much higher corruption rates. Nigeria's off-scale. At some level one might say being too human is an enormous burden.

'One might legitimately ask, what level of dark matter is beneficial to a society? I'm devoting the rest of my life to that question and I have no doubt I'll carry it unanswered to my grave. I only know it's always been with us, it's part of the dynamic of human culture. The Phoenicians had their thumbs on the scale.'

'Israel?' Lander had asked.

'Military spending distorts the model,' said Kaminsky. 'Also, so much unearned overseas remittance. I'd say Israel's pretty healthy. Good balance, dark and light matter. Personally, I'm heavily invested in Israeli stocks.'

The week droned on. The human languages multiplied. He heard himself quoted, also mocked. Some brain-mappers couldn't find any evidence of any retained consciousness even in mid-stage Alzheimer's patients, suggesting that Lander's life work was something of a fraud. Some linguists couldn't interpret Alzheimer's word-salad as anything but gibberish, thank you, Dr Lander. ('Wait'll they get hold of Kaminsky's constant in a few years,' the economist had whispered during one long, sustained attack). When the conference ended, Lander counted himself dented at the edges but basically untarnished, with important new allies.

The question that was forming was simpler than all the others: could I be happy here? Not that he feared American fascists of any colour; merely, did these cantankerous countrymen of Ari Zucker offer the completion his life had been missing? It was a question he'd never posed, could not have imagined asking at any time in his life, right up to a week before.

'Avivas?' Lander asked on the drive up to Kiryat Shimona, the last major town before the Golan. They were back to the pears. 'Aren't you afraid college kids will say "check out the Avivas on her!"?'

'I love it,' said Fisher. 'No more melons, no more hooters. Avivas!'

Lander had known these northern hills and the distant mountains forty years before, when the country was wild. You could take a gun into the hills and come back with gazelle, wild goat, even lions, some said. It was a frontier community back then with bad roads and no services, the housing was wretched, the bodies squat and faces rugged from tilling arid land between kibbutzes.

'Actually, Aviva approves. She's no prude,' said Fisher. He was a man in love, just two years into his marriage with a film-maker named Aviva Golan. The drive up from Jerusalem had begun to humanize Fisher in Lander's eyes. He was more than his pears; it's hard to begrudge a man so obviously in love. Lander's views across the board were softening. He was receptive to the dark matter within himself, within Israelis, the harshness of their views, the splits in their society that seemed only more developed than those in the States.

There had been two failed Fisher marriages, the second to a foreign service officer who'd risen more rapidly than he, got choicer postings, heavier responsibilities, a Russian specialist who saw her future in Washington and not in the field. 'You see the list of promotions and there's twenty-three women and two men – one Hispanic and one Indian, I might add – and if you squint real hard you can make out the handwriting on the wall. They offered some kind of desk job for me in Washington, but I wouldn't take it. Israel came up, I knew the language, I was interested, I looked very secular on paper which really means slightly anti-Semitic and it was just the sort of dead end job that an older man takes before retirement.'

There had been a much earlier marriage, one of those sixties things, he called it, to a Nicaraguan civilian, back in the days when it required security checks and approval all the way up the line. By the time permission came through, he'd fallen out of love, the girl and her family were lining up for favours and immigration and he'd learned that community alone is no guarantee of compatibility.

'My then-wife and I also did a sixties thing,' said Lander. 'We adopted a black baby.'

'So now she hates you?'

'She hates men and Jews and the American government in no particular order. Loves Germans, though. Calls herself Tewfiqa Niggadyke.'

'Go figure.'

'I'm giving her the title to some old family property in Berlin if she'll just change that goddamn name. We'll die out where we started, my daughter and her girlfriend. Only the colour changes.'

'No other children?'

'A catatonic monk in Japan.'

'You're really spreading the wealth.'

'You have to jab him with needles to get his attention. If a man's judged by his children, I did something wrong.'

'When I think back over my so-called career at State, I know I blew it in Nicaragua. I thought the whole Jewish Latina number was so sexy. I took a risk, it failed, it caused repercussions. Somewhere, in someone's eyes, I'm a bad risk.'

'Hello, Jonathan Pollard,' said Lander.

'Don't remind me. That *chazer* hurt us all.'

And in this way, weaving stories, establishing their expertise – for Fisher, Spanish, Russian, Hebrew and Arabic – the two drew closer, the kilometres clicked by, the land rose, the mountains drew closer, and soon they'd come to the settlement called Beth Ezra. The orchards were just beyond the fences. The Fishers' modest three rooms were inside the kibbutz, kitchen and dining were shared.

Aviva was worth waiting a lifetime for, Fisher declared in an outburst of sudden passion. The short walk from the parking space to their door was taken up in reverence for Aviva of the Pears, Aviva of the Films, Aviva of Aliyah. She too had survived bad marriages, she too had thought the time for romance in her life was over. 'What she sees in me, I don't know. You know her films, of course,' to which Lander nodded.

She was waiting at the door, a trim, indistinct, grey-haired figure with the light behind and above her. 'Hello, Gershon,' she said, the voice familiar, British. 'It's been a long time, hasn't it?'

Walls were collapsing, trees breaking with incredulity, lions, jackals, hummingbirds, 'Davia, my God!' and he melted into her arms without the consciousness of movement, two charged particles cutting through static. There were fragrances, Jaffas, tobacco, cedars and sandalwood, unlocked in an instant. Her breasts rested against him in a place untouched for forty years that unleashed tears he didn't know he had, or that anything could release. It was Lander hugging, lifting, pawing, thumping, kissing, Lander the demonstrative one, Lander the Old-World embarrassment.

'My God, dear God, oh, my God!'

She'd prepared lamb in the kibbutz kitchen with pear cobbler for dessert, good wines, fresh green beans, just-picked corn, sweet butter churned from Beth Ezra's herd of dairy cattle. Lander was shown around, no one knew him, none responded beyond the nod to America, where most had been and many had worked. It was not an English-speaking kibbutz; Lander was at a welcome disadvantage. Then they retired to the Fisher-Golan bungalow.

'My two grooms! I can't believe Dovid kept the secret!'

'Exceptionally easy, love, considering I didn't know.'

'Dovy, I told you all about Gershon. When was it, God! forty years ago?'

'A princess in '56. A queen today,' said Lander.

'I kept up with your books, you know. I was in England till about eight years ago.'

'Her husband died.'

'My third. I'm getting much better with practice.'

Practice was never her problem, Lander thought, smiling, and he could see Davia's dimples begin to flutter (he'd forgotten the dimples that made her seem so innocent, and then he remembered how she hated her dimples, who could be a serious actress with dimples?) Lander had no interest in bringing up the past, particularly if it clouded the innocence of their marriage and the earnestness David Fisher had brought to it. But, given the warmth of the greeting, the body language, how could he not know, not guess something even worse?

'Still married? Judy, isn't it?'

'You've got the name right.'

'How long?'

'Going on ten years.'

'Anyone else?'

'Not at the moment.'

'It's time to settle down, don't you think?'

'I've thought it for a long time.' Find me a Singapore economist, he thought. Find me another you.

'You don't want to face old age alone.'

'I'm facing.'

'Love, Gershon is thinking of settling. We talked about it on the ride.'

'Oh, smashing, jolly good!' she exclaimed in her best West End manner. 'You can back my films!'

'I don't know what I'd do. Keep a bag packed, get a foothold in Israel, I suppose. Seems like good advice.'

'Beware of the older women. I think they all left Miami Beach and came to Tel Aviv. There's lots of blond widows, lots of blond divorcees out there. Get a dog.'

'No dogs,' said Lander.

'Aviva thinks Jewish women get blonder as they get older.'

'It's a fact. They think it's closer to natural. Closer to white. Black would be cheating, like covering up. Blond is just … emphasizing it. So they think. I know, I've been there.'

She wasn't blond now, she was silver. She could have posed for a vitamin ad, a denture commercial, any kind of upbeat older-woman-on-a-cruise with a fit, tanned, grey-haired husband who'd looked after their investments, golfers in paradise, sailors waving to grandchildren at the dock. Not the type to make you think, however briefly, God, the cocks that had been inside her, the legions of men, the casting couches, the crews, the casts, the backers. And then himself, the boy in Israel stunned by a girl, the researcher, the young husband and father, and then the women, bodies piling up, like buses rear-ending in the fog.

'That's a complicated look, just now,' said Davia. 'If I were filming, I'd try to capture that.'

'Good thing you're not.'

The dimples fluttered.

'I think this is a miracle,' said David. 'The only word. Figure the odds.'

'I used to. Now I expect it,' said Lander. 'There are only five billion people in the world, maybe in a lifetime we see a million faces. Maybe we get to know about five thousand and we all go to the same places, hang out in the same way. I know I'll see friends in a bookstore. It would be a miracle if old friends didn't meet. Distance is no longer a factor.'

'So logical, my deah, deah boy.'

'I didn't mean a miracle-miracle.'

'Understood.'

'How about this for a miracle? You said you had a black daughter, right? I was a kind of wandering rabbi for the embassy when I was posted in Moscow. All the Jews were trying to get out, you know. Also a lot of non-Jews were trying to take advantage. I'm the guy that had to test them. So I wait till we get three or four visa applications from any given city, and I then take a visit. You know Tashkent?'

'My dau –' Lander began.

'Nasty, dry, hot place in the summer. Typical Soviet destruction of a foreign culture. So there's this guy named Shvartz, classic name, married to an American. I go, he's gone. Wife's there.'

'Black,' said Lander.

'Did I already tell this? Yeah, *shvartz* was a redundancy. No sign of him, but in perfect Russian she tells me she's an American, takes out pictures, recites –'

'– the *haftara*.'

'This is too weird.'

'Darling,' said Davia, 'I think Gershon is trying to tell you something.'

'Well, when the Soviet Union was starting to break up, you had a lot of desperate characters trapped in some pretty strange places. Somalis, Zaireans. They had forged passports, they had bribe-money, they had knives. This lady was very good –'

'Missing a finger? Spots on her hand?'

'May have. Really good English, too.'

'Coffee?' asked Davia.

'A miracle is probably a black Russian woman reciting the *haftara* in Tashkent,' said Fisher. 'Imagine the desperation of those people.'

'I'm going out for a cigarette,' she said.

'And there's the lesser miracle that she's my daughter.'

'But you said –'

'She wasn't then.'

'What about the miracle that we met? The miracle of Davia?'

'Those were just the odds, love,' she said, heading outside.

'I know,' she said. She still rolled her own. 'He's a dear, sweet man and I don't want to hear any disrespect. I will not say anything disrespectful about my husband. He was following orders. Doing his duty, that's all. What happened happened.'

'Good.'

'So she met a good woman and moved to Poland and then to Germany and lived happily ever after. But what about you?'

'I'm a survivor. I do what I have to. Don't tell him, he thinks I'm English. I've had some successes, Gershon. It makes him proud.' She stubbed her cigarette, and rolled another. All around them, outside other doors, women were standing and smoking. 'You say Jews should keep a bag packed? Think about South African Jews.'

'Too many things are collapsing, partitions are suddenly coming down.'

'It only means age, dear. The pendulous *tristesse* of breasts. Same with you, no? Cock, tummy, chin wattles, old man's earlobes ...'

'It means Judgement Day, the Messiah coming, Moloch, Armageddon, something big.'

'Dear boy. Dear, dear boy.'

The door opened.

'Catching up on old times? Look, I've been thinking. I'm sorry, I'm terribly, terribly sorry. Consular work is nine-tenths stoneheartedness, suspiciousness, saying no.'

'And being just a little bit anti-Semitic,' said Lander pleasantly. He debated saying it, and finally did. 'It's the one-tenth that judges us.' He could feel Davia's withdrawal, Fisher stiffen. 'I brought some pear brandy,' he said. 'We can have it under the trees.'

Back to Tel Aviv, the same hotel, the same sheet of white Zuckerland lights, new conferencees arriving, the old ones packing up. Lander had crammed fifty years in a week, he felt exhausted and exhilarated. Israel was so concentrated, so opinionated, so raw and so sophisticated that he felt himself returned to helpless childhood and clueless adolescence, then flung outward, into the widest reaches of maturity, weightless around a familiar planet. Only as he packed did he realize this had been a celibate conference, his first in years. Had age finally caught up with him, or did the writers clean the pool? Where were these blond divorcees, and did he really care?

Perhaps he had passed out of a phase, a long destructive one that gave back less than he put into it. If that's it, so be it.

What country do you give for a man who has everything? He longed for Ari Zucker's clarity of motive, of mission. Save my people. Lander had become a citizen of the world, Chicago more convenient than most stops, but not a burial site.

His departure was set for late the next night, time still to debate the options. In the coffee shop, where he'd least expected to find them, sat Joel Kaminsky and Angela, sharing ice cream from a silver goblet. Lander felt himself becoming the third wheel in some very strange relationships.

'My life,' he sighed, when asked his problem.

Kaminsky was reading a Hebrew newspaper, eyes darting right to left. 'What about your life, Dr Lander?' asked Angela.

'Lonely, confused, bizarre.'

'You should find a woman, before one finds you.'

'That's very sound advice,' he said.

'Not too young, however,' she went on.

'Aviva Golan's a lovely woman,' said Kaminsky. 'She told me you'd met, after many years.'

'I knew her under a different name. A different life.'

'I knew Davia when I taught at LSE. A remarkable woman. Your life's been blessed with many good friends, Gerald.'

'You probably know Ari Zucker, too.'

'I knew him as Arnie, but yes, I advised some friends of his a long time ago. It turned out well for everybody.'

'This country's one family, isn't it?'

'On our level, yes. I don't know the new Russians, I don't know many north Africans. The Yemenis are a mystery.'

'Could I be happy here?'

'Why not stay back a day or two? Make inquiries. I can give you names. They have a saying here. An Israeli should keep his bag packed. Don't give up your Chicago place.'

And so it happened two days later that Lander didn't take his ticketed flight. He wondered, as he often did, if by ditching the flight he'd reshuffled his diminishing deck, brought the fatal card closer to the top, or buried it deeper. Tomorrow would he wake to the news of a terrible crash, or would the fated crash now be his, whenever he took it? His son, the Enlightened One, would have something to say, if prodded, about destiny and the afterlife, about ego, the futility of attachment to the flesh, the mind, the career.

One more book, one more decade, anticipation and memory, all the binaries, all the plays and novels and poems that fed into it, all the religious texts, the dark and light matter of the universe, the solitary pleasure of writing. He had already wasted so much of his life, spent so much energy in pursuit of ... ego, the flesh, ambition. He walked to the lobby, glad to be unrecognized, picking his way through mounds of luggage, groups of Americans and Japanese, a few local businessmen in untucked shirts and pocket calculators meeting with dark-suited Japanese, a sign in Hebrew which, miraculously, he could read. 'Cohens May Enter,' it said, meaning safe for priests, whatever food or services lay behind it.

Things coming back. The tide washing in. A man lowered a Hebrew newspaper, slowly, as though afraid of what he might see, and Lander recognized him as well, his ancient double, the man in a dream of so many years. What to do now but smile, and make the hands-out, palms-up gesture familiar to them both? But the man panicked and bolted from the chair, dropping the newspaper. The front of the hotel was blocked by baggage; the double took the side-entrance, nearly running through the glass door. 'It's all right,' Lander wanted to cry out, 'it's just the odds, nothing more.'

He thought of himself suddenly as a zebra in the short grass of the African *veldt*, one among an identical many. He thought of lionesses, of hyenas, the leap of an enormous weight upon his back, teeth clamped about his neck. He couldn't breathe, the air was turning purple. The purple of his algebra vision so many years before, the purple light of discovery when his mother's words became explicable. He was surprised he could even stagger under such a weight, that no one in the registration line had turned in astonishment at such a sight, a zebra in sandals and a loose white shirt, in the lobby of a fancy hotel, attacked by lions.

And then the shadow he'd been pursuing these past ten years suddenly took on substance. It was all so simple, really, the beautiful vision, the unified field theory. It was the lion. His life's work wasn't the final thing; it was only the beginning. The brain is wired for thousands of applications, not just for speech and spotty recall, but for clairvoyance and telepathy and a thousand other higher powers. Our tragedy is profound – we've lost the access codes. We've invented excuses, like time, to symbolize the unknown. Language is our pale compensation, porpoise calls and wolf howls, for the loss of our true humanity. Language is fax instead of e-mail, an electric typewriter instead of a word processor. The embedded syntactical structures of our brain are too complex for mere language. Language is a primitive lung, an evolutionary stage.

What chemical, stored in the deepest fold of the primitive brain was being released at just that moment, what protein of recognition allowed the zebra, the wildebeest, the house cat slinking to the basement corner, to enter his final moments convinced of the futility of escape? The dominance of our species has been purchased with the capital of our brains' own wiring.

They live in the moment, we say of animals and of people we depict as primitive, of Alzheimer's patients. It seemed an exquisite profundity. What does it mean, *to live in the moment*?

This would be his work, in the time remaining.

He went outside, across the portico to the corner to stare at the wall of Zuckerland's cold white light, brighter than a thousand suns. He did not notice – no one did – a gleaming Mercedes parked in front. But a man walking past did look in, did stoop, and then began to run. Others coming out of Zuckerland carrying appliances, Lander at the corner about to go back inside, the kids flipping through CDs, the bus honking and then unloading around the illegally parked car, the tourists in the lobby, none of them noticed, none of them heard the warnings of one crazy man running and shouting hysterically. No one had a chance when the car mysteriously hiccuped and a fireball erupted. Its windows blew out and the fireball expanded. The street shook, shards of fluorescent tubing lifted and propelled themselves, light as balloons in every direction, to radiate in a pattern like a glittering fence around the crater, the bodies, the luggage, the bus and the front half of the hotel.

It was all caught on satellite footage, the calm day, the city far below, '... and now,' announcers around the world intoned, 'watch for a bright light in the lower left. Keep watching, and you'll see the wave of destruction.'

Many commentators picked up on the irony that if one small shred of hope can be gleaned from such a catastrophe it might be this: that had the bomb gone off just thirty-six hours earlier, it would have eliminated the greatest collection of minds ever assembled in one place in the past half century.

Dear Gershon, the letter read, opened by a postal clerk and sold to investigators many months later. *I cannot rest tonight, not after the way we behaved. You were a gentleman to me always, my knight as the years wore on and it seemed there were no heroes left. Seeing you again, not being able to hold you, to be held by you, has broken my heart in ways I did not think possible in one so old, and presumably, so accustomed to heartbreak (and, you're probably thinking because I can read your face, heart breaking). You were going to stay in Israel, but after our behaviour how could we expect you to? How could I? This morning we awoke to the terrible news of the bomb that went off in front of your hotel; if you'd stayed, you surely would be no more. I take the smallest satisfaction possible that something started in Tashkent and revealed in Beth Ezra may have, in some bizarre twist, saved your life. For that, I thank* G-D. *All my love, Davia.*

EPILOGUE

Yahrzeit

From our Tel Aviv correspondent, affiliates please copy ...

As Israel prepares to mourn more than six hundred deaths one year after the Black Tuesday bombing, speculation deepens over the whereabouts of renowned psycholinguist Gerald Lander, last seen in public just minutes before the blast.

Lander is best known for his groundbreaking work on Alzheimer's disease, and for applications of his theories to the treatment of schizophrenia, autism and other brain disorders.

The Black Tuesday bombing of downtown Tel Aviv is the bloodiest terrorist act of modern times, exceeding in carnage the 331 deaths in the bombing of two Air India 747s, allegedly by Sikh terrorists, some dozen years ago.

No linkage, however, has been established between Lander's disappearance and the bombing. Local intelligence authorities have discounted the possibility of foul play or political abduction, despite claims of his captivity and demands for the release of prisoners by Muslim groups under Iranian control. Such claims have been labelled fantasies by Israeli intelligence.

Nevertheless, even well-connected authorities in Israel and the United States agree that the situation is far from resolution. Dr Lander has missed lectures, appointments and travel dates, including major addresses in Paris, Berlin, Tokyo and New York. More disturbing to investigators, his apartment rent has not been paid, his piled-up mail occupies a 'Lander room' in the Chicago post office, bills are unpaid, cheques uncashed and personal letters unopened.

'It's like he died,' said the building superintendant who still faithfully waters plants and does minimal dusting. The police are in agreement, after APBs and Interpol failed to turn up a trace of his whereabouts.

'I'd feel better about this if he'd taken some simple precautions,' said a high-ranking official of the Chicago Police Department. 'He's an adult, we can't go looking for him without cause. But no rent cheques, no mail pickup, no cancellations – this has the earmarks of foul play.'

He is, apparently, a man who has lived a year without using his credit cards or cashing a traveller's cheque. New York attorney Judy Miller, his former wife, is as shocked as anyone. 'It's not like him,' she said, citing his social habits, and their own frequent contact which she states has been broken. 'The man's everywhere. He has friends all over the world, he's a restless traveller. I can't imagine him going underground and settling somewhere. He even drops in on friends at their public lectures, anywhere in the world. It gets to where people leave tickets for Lander the way they do for Elvis. It breaks my heart to say this, but I fear,' she concluded.

'It would be harder to hide him than Salman Rushdie,' added his editor in New York, who has had long experience with both Lander and the India-born Rushdie, still under death-threat for 'blashpemy'. 'A Thomas Pynchon or J.D. Salinger [authors well-known for their reclusiveness] he's not.'

Two eyewitnesses, a married couple from New York who wish to remain anonymous, affirm that they saw Gerald Lander, a famous face, after all, flee to safety. 'He jumped out of his chair as though he'd had a vision,' claims one witness, who was nearly knocked over by the man now the subject of worldwide concern. Other witnesses, part of a late-arriving Canadian group who left the lobby discouraged by long check-in lines, swear he stayed behind. 'I saw him sitting there big as life and wanted to get his signature,' said Mrs Betty Nicholson of Montreal.

Credible reports of other sightings are abundant in Tel Aviv, where the nature of this state, and society, makes anonymity next to impossible.

Positioning at ground zero is all important; there are no known survivors from the hotel lobby, its street-facing rooms, or from adjacent buildings.

Further, to urban dailies …

Latest speculation centres on the possibility that Dr Lander, world-famous for his inquiries into the languages of mental disorder and deterioration, has absented himself deliberately and even changed his name as a prelude to immigration to Israel. Security, privacy and perhaps a deep personality change are cited as possible motivations. He is known to have been working on new applications to his theories, elaborated in a talk delivered in Jerusalem the same week of his disappearance, that hinted broadly at the possibility of tapping linguistic potential, or, as he had put it, 'a unified theory of language de-acquisition, and what it might suggest of older, but still powerful brain structures.'

Fellow researchers have always acknowledged Lander's contributions to fundamental thinking about language and consciousness even as they divide over their strict application. 'He is the last of the great nineteenth-century rational humanists,' stated Dr Karen Toomey of the University of California at Berkeley, 'he never questioned that reason could unlock and decode any irrationality, or that the human soul, if I may use so quaint a nineteenth-century term, could ever be exterminated. And if I may add a personal note, he is a charming, even playful, always fearless researcher.'

In a recent publication of 'Lander Reassessments' (Harvard University Press, Dalal and Gordon, editors), Dr Kenji Wakamatsu of Tokyo Neurolinguistic Institute likened the 'Landerian brain's' untapped resources to ever more powerful computers, whose technical capacities may run ahead of their users' ingenuity. 'What programmes we input, the brain can run. Landerian theories support the notion that structures exist in the brain which are passed through language itself, as though language were the brain's DNA.' Pressed further on that point, Dr Wakamatsu suggested that the brain might indeed be 'wired' for telepathy and clairvoyance, in much the way it is for language acquisition and the storage of memory. 'We must ask, as Lander does, what language is. Words are like fibre optics, their carrying capacity has barely been explored.'

For that reason, others, like the leftist French social linguist Marcel Feininger, suggest, 'the corruption and coarsening of language, notably through mass-appeal television, can, over time, desensitize the transmission of the capacity for thought itself.'

Dr Prakash Dalal, co-editor of the Harvard University Press volume, states in his introduction, 'When we assess Gerald Lander, we clearly re-assess Freud, but less directly, we re-indebt ourselves to Einstein, to Darwin, to Ramanujan. It was the unaided human brain working nearly alone without basic calculators let alone computers that devised theories that our most advanced telescopes and microscopes are only now confirming; that hinted at the existence of such exotic and seemingly irrational concepts as black holes, binary systems and dark matter, or, as in the case of Darwin, that made sense of mad abundance, useless replication and mindless variation, that eventually broke down the rigid orthodoxy of time itself. Today we treat the universe in its incomprehensible scale as an evolutionary event. Tomorrow we may do the same for the brain and its link to consciousness.'

His friends even arranged a well-publicized Lander Roast this spring, thinking to lure him back into the spotlight, in which the biggest names in the field signed on for a 'Gerald Lander, Prophet or Fraud?' fifteen-year assessment of the so-called Lander Revolution. He did not appear. A lecture in Paris two weeks later was held open until the last minute, the crowd that was turned away that night at the Sorbonne is said to rival that mobilized for rare lectures by *les immortels* or the latest intellectual craze. Perhaps in Berlin, the cry went up, but Berlin was cancelled as well.

His daughter, Tewfiqa Lander, contacted at her home in Berlin, said the last communication from her father had been a card from Israel, which she agreed to share with reporters. *Dear Tewfie and S_____; I am well, and much excited by a new project which must remain very hush-hush. Incidentally, I met the man who changed your life in Tashkent. On our behalf, and at some personal cost, I did not forgive him. Love, Daddy.* The references remain vague at this time and attempts to access Embassy files have been blocked at the highest level. The Landers have a son, last reported to be in a Buddhist retreat in Japan, who could not be contacted for this article.

The Nobel Prize-winning economist, Joel Kaminsky, who last saw Lander in Jerusalem at a Human Languages conference, and then later in Tel Aviv on the Sunday preceding the blast, confirmed the impression that Lander might still be in Israel, working in deep privacy on problems of a personal and professional nature.

'Gerry Lander is well connected in Israel,' said Kaminsky from his home in New York, 'there are people who would shield him if he wished to avoid the public. Kaminsky's major work, *In Praise of Corruption*, was known to have influenced much of Lander's later thinking on so-called anticipation theory, which some regard as the 'disused pathway' (Kaminsky calls it 'the rabbit hole, like Alice's plunge into Wonderland') that could open up an unmapped neurolinguistic universe.

Asked if he had been given a hint of Lander's latest undertaking, the 84-year-old economist said, 'It will be revolutionary. It will do for all of us, even functioning geriatrics such as myself, what his first book did for the so-called senile demented. He has discovered a power of the brain that was always there but never tapped. Something we left behind.'

There continues to be speculation, now hardening to firm belief in many circles, that Gerald Lander was one of the dozens of unidentified victims of the Black Tuesday blast. He could have left the hotel but circled back. 'Maybe he forgot something, maybe he wanted to make a phone call, whatever,' said an old Brooklyn friend, Ari Zucker, now a Tel Aviv resident. Zucker, owner of the appliance store directly at ground zero had himself been delayed at home that Tuesday morning. He says now, 'I torture myself. Maybe he was coming back to see me, have a coffee or something.'

A check of airline departures discloses that Lander had cancelled his original departure date, which would have placed him safely back in the U.S. at the time of the Tel Aviv tragedy. His personal and professional appointments on that last morning in Tel Aviv are all well-known and exhaustively documented. Dr Zvi Cohen, director of neurolinguistics at the Hebrew University of Jerusalem, acknowledged that Dr Lander had been in contact regarding the offer of a permanent research residency. But Israel immigration authorities have no record of his application for Israeli residence and citizenship. Diasporic American Jews, like Dr Lander, are routinely admitted to Israel and permitted dual citizenship by both countries.

The irony that Gerald Lander might have perished in a blast triggered by fringe elements in a tribal conflict that has nearly been resolved by political means would be grotesque, a tragedy for all who read his work and honour its lucidity, and who dare to think they had an ally in the highest reaches of science, someone who thought for them, lived for them, believed in them.

Plans are being laid in the United States and in Israel, with contributions from publishers, foundations and researchers in nearly every country where Gerald Lander lectured or counselled patients, to endow a permanent facility in neurolinguistics in his name should his death, the last of the Black Tuesday tragedies, ever be proven.

Clark Blaise was born in Fargo, North Dakota, in 1940 to French and Anglophone-Canadian parents. He moved often during his childhood years as the family followed the disastrous fortunes of his furniture salesman father. Blaise graduated from Denison University in Granville, Ohio in 1961 and then went to Harvard to study writing with Bernard Malamud. In 1962 he moved to attend the Univerisity of Iowa's Writers' Workshop where he met and married the well-known American novelist Bharati Mukherjee.

He emigrated to Montreal in 1966 in search of his French-Canadian roots and taught for the next twelve years at Sir George Williams University where he established what is now Concordia's creative writing workshop.

After a brief period at York University, Clark and Bharati moved back to the United States where Clark is now Director of the prestigious International Writing Program at Iowa.